Praise for the Christiansen Family Series

It Had to Be You

"*It Had to Be You* is a sigh-worthy, coming-into-her-own romance highlighting the importance of family, the necessity of faith, and how losing yourself for the right reasons can open your heart to something beautiful."

SERENA CHASE, *USA TODAY*

"This character-driven tale with a beautiful love story . . . gives excellent spiritual insight and a gorgeously written look at what it means to surrender and let go."

ROMANTIC TIMES

"Susan May Warren delivers another beautiful, hope-filled story of faith that makes the reader fall further in love with this captivating and intriguing family. . . . Powerful storytelling gripped me from beginning to end . . . [and] lovable characters ensure that the reader becomes invested in their lives."

RADIANT LIT

"This is one author who is only getting better with each book, and I cannot wait to find out which character we are next invited to meet in this Christiansen family."

FICTION ADDICT

"A gem of a story, threaded with truth and hope, laughter and romance. Susan May Warren brings the Christiansen family to life, as if they might be my family or yours, with her smooth writing and engaging storytelling."

RACHEL HAUCK, bestselling author of *The Wedding Dress*

Take a Chance on Me

"Warren's new series launch has it all: romance, suspense, and intrigue. It is sure to please her many fans and win her new readers, especially those who enjoy Terri Blackstock."

LIBRARY JOURNAL

"Warren . . . has crafted an engaging tale of romance, rivalry, and the power of forgiveness."

PUBLISHERS WEEKLY

"Warren once again creates a compelling community full of vivid individuals whose anguish and dreams are so real and relatable, readers will long for every character to attain the freedom their hearts desire."

BOOKLIST

"*Take a Chance on Me* is the first of six books in this new series from prolific author Susan May Warren—and I couldn't be more excited! I've already fallen in love with the Christiansen family . . . and I can't wait to see how Warren brings true and lasting love into the lives of Darek's two brothers and three sisters."

SERENA CHASE, *USA TODAY*

"A compelling story of forgiveness and redemption, *Take a Chance on Me* will have readers taking a chance on each beloved character!"

CBA RETAILERS + RESOURCES

"Warren's latest is a touching tale of love discovered and the meaning of family."

ROMANTIC TIMES

EVERGREEN

a Christiansen winter novella

Evergreen

SUSAN MAY WARREN

Christy Award—winning author

Tyndale House Publishers, Inc.
Carol Stream, Illinois

Visit Tyndale online at www.tyndale.com.

Visit Susan May Warren's website at www.susanmaywarren.com.

TYNDALE and Tyndale's quill logo are registered trademarks of Tyndale House Publishers, Inc.

Evergreen

Designed by Jennifer Phelps

Edited by Sarah Mason

Published in association with the literary agency of The Steve Laube Agency, 5025 N. Central Ave., #635, Phoenix, AZ 85012.

Evergreen is a work of fiction. Where real people, events, establishments, organizations, or locales appear, they are used fictitiously. All other elements of the novel are drawn from the author's imagination.

Library of Congress Cataloging-in-Publication Data

Warren, Susan May, date.
  Evergreen / Susan May Warren.
    pages cm. — (Christiansen family)
    ISBN 978-1-4143-9401-5 (hc)
1. Clergy—Fiction. 2. Empty nesters—Fiction. 3. Older couples—Fiction.
4. Minnesota—Fiction. 5. Domestic fiction. I. Title.
PS3623.A865E935 2014
  813'.6—dc23   2014014099

Printed in the United States of America

20	19	18	17	16	15	14
7	6	5	4	3	2	1

For Your glory, Lord

ACKNOWLEDGMENTS

WITH EVERY BOOK I WRITE, I'm aware of my need to have a supportive team to pull the story together. I'm so grateful for the brilliance and inspiration from the following people:

Rachel Hauck, who knows exactly the right questions to ask as she walks through every chapter with me.

Ellen Tarver, my first reader, who understands story and knows how to fix the broken ones.

Karen Watson, my editor, along with Stephanie Broene. Thank you for partnering with me to create the magic of the Christiansens.

Sarah Mason, who adds shine and polish.

Special thanks also go to Joyce and Eric Warren for letting us borrow their amazing son, Seth, for a year. What a blessing to be a part of his life journey!

And Seth, of course, my favorite nephew. I fully expect you to go and be awesome.

My Noah, who came up with the fire and many other Romeo moments. You are one of my favorites.

Sarah and Neil, a reminder of the joy of the beginning. I am so excited about your tomorrows.

And Pete, my independent one, Christmas tree enthusiast, the keeper of traditions. The party doesn't truly start until you arrive.

My David, story crafter extraordinaire. Seriously. Wow.

My Andrew, who keeps our marriage evergreen. Hey, look—they're gone! When are we going to Prague?

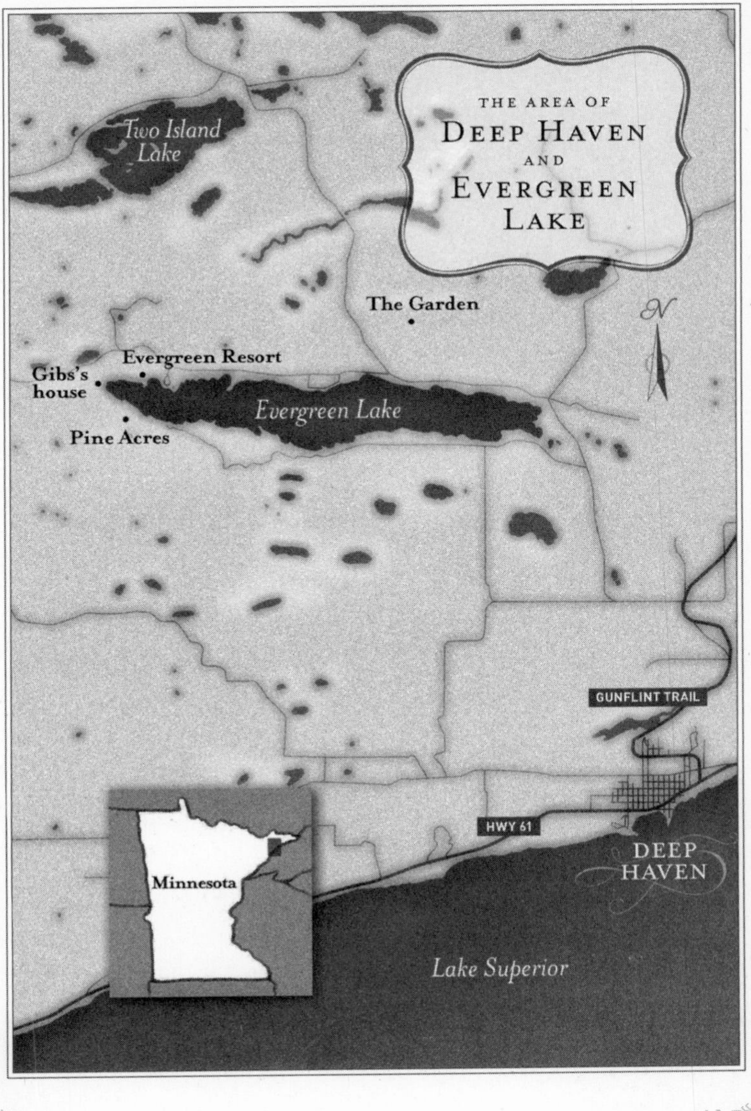
THE AREA OF
DEEP HAVEN
AND
EVERGREEN
LAKE
Two Island Lake
The Garden
N
Evergreen Resort
Gibs's house
Evergreen Lake
Pine Acres
GUNFLINT TRAIL
HWY 61
DEEP HAVEN
Minnesota
Lake Superior

Dear family and friends,

A warm Christmas greeting from the Christiansen family in snowy northern Minnesota.

We've had a year of joy as each of the family has found new adventures. Darek and Ivy tied the knot last Memorial Day, and Eden and Jace Jacobsen followed with a celebration in August. Casper has moved to Roatán to work on a sunken galleon in pursuit of his archaeology degree . . .

Dear family and friends,

A warm Christmas greeting from the Christiansen family in snowy northern Minnesota.

The Christiansen family has seen much change this year. We've worked hard on the resort, and it is nearly rebuilt after last year's devastating forest fire. Grace is finally pursuing her love of cooking, working as a chef in Minneapolis and looking forward to marrying NHL hockey player Maxwell Sharpe. Meanwhile, Owen has been out west, fighting fires with a hotshot team. We were all delighted when he showed up for Eden's wedding . . .

Dear family and friends,

A warm Christmas greeting from the Christiansen family in snowy northern Minnesota.

It's a year of new beginnings for us as our children start new chapters in their lives. We are thrilled to have sent Amelia off to Prague for her first year of college . . .

Dear family and friends,

A warm Christmas greeting from the Christiansen family in snowy northern Minnesota!

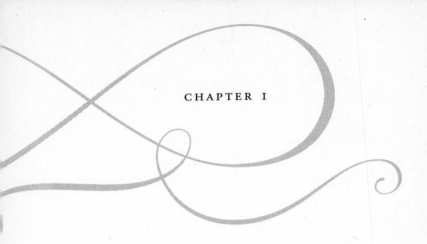

CHAPTER I

OF ALL THE DAYS for the pastor to expound past the allotted time for his sermon, he had to pick potluck day. The day of the quarterly business meeting.

The day of the Minnesota Vikings home opener—against the Green Bay Packers, no less.

John Christiansen stood in the buffet line of the fellowship hall and glanced at the clock hanging over the pass-through to the church kitchen. He did a quick calculation. If he skipped the dessert line and another cup of coffee, and if he planted himself next to his best friend, Nathan Decker—who could run interference between John and the entanglements of mindless conversation about the unusual Minnesotan warm snap this late into September—he just might make it home before the end of the first quarter.

He'd give Nate his voting proxy for any sudden decisions at the meeting. Yes, he'd agree to be a Salvation Army bell ringer at the grocery store this Christmas. No, he didn't think the church needed to hire a snowplowing service—he'd be glad to come down with his truck again this year. Or to send his oldest son, Darek, over. It seemed about time Darek inherited that duty too.

John guessed he had about seventeen minutes to effect his escape before Pastor Dan rose and trapped him in a two-hour meeting that he'd gladly trade for having his fingernails plucked out with a pair of snub-nosed pliers.

But it all hinged on catching his wife with the hairy eyeball of desperation.

Sadly, Ingrid had planted herself with her back to him, holding a plate of food, talking to Ellie, Pastor Dan's wife.

He tried not to accuse his wife of being diabolical.

"Oh, good, there are meatballs left." Nate reached over from the opposite side of the buffet table. "I love Ingrid's barbecue meatballs."

"It's her hockey-mom potluck specialty," John said, scooping into the garlic mashed potatoes.

"I'm glad she decided to share it with the church," Nathan said. "Can't let all those fabulous potluck recipes go to waste, even if the high school hockey years are over."

He added mashed potatoes to his own plate. "So how are your honeymooners doing?"

John glanced at Ingrid, seeing her move on from her small talk with Ellie. She looked pretty today in a pink sweater and floral skirt, her blonde hair pulled back with a headband. Sometimes she looked as fresh and young as when he'd first noticed her, thirty-some years ago.

Yeah, she still possessed the power to unravel him, steal his thoughts, turn his mouth dry.

He nearly called across the room for her to save him a seat, but that felt too desperate. She didn't look at him, stopping to chat with Edith Draper, head of the hospitality committee.

Danger! Danger! He nearly abandoned his meatballs right there and made a dash for his wife.

But after nearly thirty years of marriage, she knew not to volunteer him for any committees or projects, right?

Somehow he managed to keep a cool head and answer Nate, updating him on the status of his adult children.

"Eden and Jace are looking at houses in Minneapolis. Hitting the parade of homes. Grace's fiancé, Max, survived hockey camp. They have a preseason game coming up in a few weeks. And Grace is working on her catering business."

"They set a date yet?"

Oh, good, Ingrid had laughed, shaken her head, and walked away from Edith, looking for an open space to sit in the crowded fellowship hall.

The claws in John's chest loosened.

"Nope. I wouldn't be surprised if they had their wedding in Hawaii."

"That sounds expensive." Nathan handed John a roll of silverware. John took it, balancing it under his plate filled with potatoes, green beans, meatballs, corn salad, and a few items he didn't quite know how to name.

"Maybe. But Max has money. After all, he does play for the NHL." He noticed Ingrid had taken a chair next to Helen Harrison, Nathan's mother. No danger there. Helen headed up the Christmas decorating committee, but even if Ingrid did suddenly decide he'd be perfect to cut and put up the church's tree, it still wouldn't interfere with any of John's plans.

He set his plate on a table, slid out a folding chair. Nate sat next to him.

"Have you heard from Casper?" Nate asked without looking at him, unrolling his napkin.

Only a handful of people knew about the Christiansen family debacle the morning of Eden and Jace's wedding—the fistfight between his two younger sons, Owen and Casper.

"He's living on some Caribbean island and loving his new gig working on an archaeology team for the winter." Or at least that's what he made it sound like. But John had the sense that he hadn't gotten the full story from Casper in years.

"Fun. I remember when we used to dream of traveling. Nice to know your kids are actually doing it, huh?"

Actually doing it . . . Well, maybe Nate could keep a secret. John kept his voice low. "I'm booking a trip for Ingrid and me to Europe over Christmas."

There, he'd said it out loud. Made it real. Actually put words to the idea that had been simmering inside him since they'd said good-bye to Amelia, their youngest child, two weeks ago at the Minneapolis–St. Paul International Airport.

Nate looked away, then back to John as if trying to comprehend his words. "Seriously?"

Okay, so he'd known the idea could be risky, but . . . "Listen, Ingrid is always saying she'd like to travel, and I thought with Amelia over in Prague this semester, and with all the other kids busy . . . it's perfect. We'll be back in time to get ready for the resort grand opening over Valentine's weekend, and I've been tucking money away for years. It feels like it's now or never."

Nate smiled. "It's fantastic, man. I'd love to escape with Annalise for the holidays, but she'd kill me. Too many traditions."

"We have traditions too, but this year the kids have plans, with the exception of Darek and Ivy—and they're celebrating their first Christmas as a family—so it seems like we'll be largely on our own. Ingrid's been acting sort of . . . down, ever since the wedding."

"And you think tickets to Europe are going to fix everything?"

"Of course. Why not?" He finished off his last meatball. His wife could cook with the best of them—probably where Grace got her culinary skills. "I thought it could be a sort of second honeymoon." He looked at his plate. "I'm planning to take her to the top of the Eiffel Tower and renew our vows."

Nate shook his head. "Who knew? John Christiansen is a romantic."

"I'm going to pretend you didn't say that." But maybe, down deep, he could be. Sweep his wife off her feet, just like he had once upon a time. "I figure, we raised our kids, and now it's time for us, right?"

Nate grinned, lifted his glass. "You're the man."

Yeah. That's right. "I'm buying the tickets tomorrow—"

"Grandpa!"

John turned as Tiger ran up to him. The six-year-old flung his arms around his neck. "Am I comin' over to watch the game?"

"Absolutely—"

"Sorry, buddy." This from Ivy, John's daughter-in-law. She wore a pretty lime green–and–brown dress and had tied her red hair back in a green scarf. She came up behind Tiger, holding a jacket, so easily moving into the role of stepmom that it seemed she'd been handpicked by God to fill the void left by Tiger's mother's death. "Grandpa has to stay for a church meeting."

Shoot. How obvious would it be now for him to sneak out? He glanced at Ingrid again and tried not to harbor the belief that she was intentionally ignoring him.

By now, the Vikings had probably surrendered at least one touchdown.

He spied movement from Pastor Dan, making his way to the front.

Beside him, Nate laughed. "I just hope you taped the game, pal."

John grimaced and reached for the coffee carafe.

Dan led them in prayer. John visited the dessert table during the reading of the minutes, tried to get the score on his phone, and nodded a few times at the discussion of a men's community Bible study.

He signed his name on the pass-along sheet for Salvation Army volunteers and then on a whim added Ingrid's name, just in case she tried to sign up separately. If he worked it out right, they could be at the airport by the evening of December 23.

He'd already planned the surprise in his mind—he'd spring the gift on her at Thanksgiving. He didn't know what the head count might be for that weekend, and she just might be feeling glum. The thought of her elation made the details of the hospitality report bearable.

"On to new business," Edith said. "Our church is hosting the annual community live Nativity this year."

Oh no. He made a face at Nathan, who mimicked it. John cut his voice low. "Another tradition I'll be glad to miss."

Nathan nodded. "Last year I think we did a drive-by, saw maybe a handful of families out there. Remember the year we replaced the baby Jesus with a ham?"

John laughed, earning a death glare from Ingrid. The live Nativity display might hold a fascination for a dwindling handful, but he'd spent too many hours, from his childhood and beyond, standing in the cold, bulwarking a tradition the town should have let crumble long ago.

And then it happened.

Edith turned to Ingrid, and in his beautiful wife's face John saw an expression that ignited a dark, twining horror. He barely bit back the impulse to leap up, take a run at old Edith the troublemaker, and tackle her and her clipboard before she could utter another word.

But convention rooted him to his chair, cold fingers digging into his chest as Edith smiled at Ingrid and said, "I have in our records that John and Ingrid are signed up to coordinate it."

No! The fingers clamped down, choking off his words, when he saw Ingrid nod. "Of course. We'll be happy to."

She didn't even look at him.

Do something. The voice careened through his head as Edith moved on to other items, something about the Christmas tea—

"Wait!" The word emerged faintly high, sounding woefully unlike his own voice.

Even Nate turned, his expression so vivid, John could hear him behind the chaos of his panic, warning him off. If only he were a good listener. "Do we have to actually *be* there for the live Nativity, or can we just organize it?"

A hush vised the room, and John's heartbeat pulsed in his ears.

Edith frowned. "I . . . well, I suppose not. As long as all the roles are filled."

"Thank you, Edith. We'll make sure the parts are filled and everything is perfect."

"Oh." She pressed a hand to her chest as if to pat her heart back into place. "Okay, then."

He refused to surrender. He did, however, glance at Ingrid.

Her lips froze in a forced smile, her jaw drawn so tight he thought she might be grinding molars.

"Way to do an end run," Nate said quietly. He made a fist and held it out for a congratulatory bump.

John met it. Yeah, that's right. Nothing—not even Ingrid—would stop him from giving his wife the best Christmas of her life.

If John wanted any hope of seeing his stupid football game, he'd better stop hanging around the church kitchen, looking at his watch.

And his phone.

And the clock.

As if the Vikings might be waiting for him to show up and save the day with a fourth-quarter eighty-yard run.

From his armchair.

Ingrid sprayed more water on her baking pan and attacked the barbecue residue with renewed vigor. Around her, other ladies on the hospitality committee finished unloading the commercial dishwasher, packing up leftovers, and cleaning out the coffeepots.

"You know who would make a good couple for the Nativity display is Ivy and Darek," Annalise Decker was saying as she emptied the load of clean silverware into a drawer. "Although maybe we should wait a year for them— by then they might have a live baby to lay in the manger."

Ingrid glanced at her and found a smile. "Maybe." Another grandbaby. The thought really should seed some warmth in her heart, but . . .

Well, since that day when her family fell apart, when she saw her two youngest sons brawling on the morning of her daughter's wedding, a slow chill had turned everything inside her to January.

And Mr. Hurry-up-or-I'll-miss-the-game wasn't helping. She'd wanted the floor to open up and take her when he suggested not being around for the live Nativity.

Not that she felt especially keen on coordinating and

staffing the town's feeble hold on the tradition either. In years past, the entire town of Deep Haven had gathered on Christmas Eve for a moment of community solidarity, with carols and a cookie exchange. However, every year fewer showed up to celebrate. And why not? Everyone was leaving home, lives changing.

No one wanted to stand around for an hour in the snow, watching a mock Mary and Joseph shiver in the cold.

"Are you all right, Ingrid?"

"Yes. I'm just thinking about the live Nativity."

"It's so sad that no one attends anymore. Pastor Dan was saying that the ecumenical board nearly voted to discontinue it. Maybe they will if we don't get anyone to attend this year." Annalise picked up a towel. "I remember my first Christmas in Deep Haven. The live Nativity felt so fresh to me. I'd never truly understood the story before. If only we could figure out a way to put new life into it."

"I just hope it doesn't storm like it did a few years ago."

"And that we can keep the angels from fighting." Annalise winked at her, and Ingrid's memory returned to a chilly night long ago when she discovered Casper and Owen, dressed in sheets, wrestling in the snow, their wings cast off and bent.

Acid filled her chest as she mustered up a smile, cheery

words. "Who knows? Maybe it'll be the best live Nativity ever." She turned back to the pan. "I don't know why I forgot to line this pan with foil, but I think it'll take a chisel and hammer to get this barbecue sauce off."

"Let it soak at home, honey," John said from the door.

She ignored him and the edge of impatience in his tone. The Vikings rarely won a game against the Packers. Fighting words hung on her lips, but—

No. Marriage called for patience. Especially for football widows.

"I've nearly got it."

"Leave it here," Annalise said. "It does need to soak, and you can pick it up tomorrow at women's Bible study." She handed Ingrid a towel, glanced at John. "Go Vikings."

"Rah," Ingrid said, but she gathered her purse and followed John from the church.

Outside, the afternoon sun cast shadows across the dirt parking lot, and the loamy tang of autumn seasoned with the piney tartness of the north shore scented the air. The church overlooked the deep-indigo waters of Lake Superior, the clouds thin and high. Another week or so and the days might start turning cool, but for now, they beckoned her out onto her deck to read, or to the dock to watch the loons paddle in the lake.

Ingrid climbed into the truck. She didn't need John to shut the door after her but smiled in his direction anyway when he did. No reason to pick a fight.

John backed out of the lot. "I thought I'd swing by Darek's and maybe we'd finish the game there."

Darek had moved to town with his new bride, Ivy—at John's suggestion, of course—beginning the transformation of her house into a tomb. Then Grace moved to Minneapolis to be closer to her fiancé, Max. And in the two weeks since Amelia's departure, the morose quietness of their resort home had begun to press like mud into her bones, turning every day a little swampy and thick.

"We need to get home. Butter has been trapped in the house all morning, and she needs to go out."

John glanced at her.

Ingrid didn't have to actually turn her head to see it; after nearly thirty years, she could predict his movements, read his mind. "I left her in the house for church because I thought it might rain," she added.

"She's a dog."

"She's a sixteen-year-old dog."

"She can wait."

"John, be fair. She's house-trained, and she won't go inside. Which means she's going to be in pain. Or worse, she'll piddle on the floor and be upset. Her bladder isn't what it used to be. Do you want to clean it up?"

John sighed. "Maybe it's time to think of putting—"

"John! We are not putting Butter to sleep."

He frowned. "I was going to say putting in a dog door."

Oh.

"Well, I don't think it's so much to ask to go home to let her out. You can watch the rest of the game from there."

"If there's any of it left."

She heard the mumble, although he probably hadn't tried to disguise it. "Sorry. But I think it is important to keep our commitments. We are members. We should attend the business meetings." *And do our part to run the Christmas Nativity.*

"I wish you hadn't volunteered us for that Nativity project." Apparently he could read her mind too.

"I saw you put my name down for the Salvation Army—"

"That's different. It's one hour, maybe two. And we can do it together."

She shot him a look. "Aren't you going to help me with the live Nativity?"

He sighed, and she braced herself. But his soft tone unseated her. "It's just that . . . I was hoping we'd . . ." His hands tightened around the steering wheel as they turned off the main highway onto their road toward Evergreen Lake.

At his stalled words, she looked at him, frowning. Hoping they'd . . . what?

The low-hanging sun, the gold cascading through the cab of the truck, illuminated, just for a moment, the man he'd been, the one full of hopes, dreams. His wide shoulders still strong from his football days, built lean and tough and ready to conquer the world for her.

He'd fed her with stories of the life they'd build together and beyond. Hopes of family and adventure. And he'd given her most of it. Enough of it, at least. Then why, suddenly, since Amelia walked out the door, did she feel so empty?

She wanted to blame it on the recent fight between her children. Or simply the melancholy of being left behind as her children launched into their lives.

Yes, certainly that was it.

He sighed again. "Of course I'll help you with the live Nativity."

Ingrid looked away at the litter of bejeweled leaves scattered along the ditch of the dirt road. "You don't need to help, John." In fact, she didn't need him to have the best live Nativity scene Deep Haven had ever seen.

They pulled up to the house and he got out. She didn't wait for him to open the door but headed inside.

Butterscotch met them at the door, whining, and shot past Ingrid the moment she opened it.

Ingrid dumped her purse on the bench by the door, and John headed toward the den.

She heard the cheers of the game before she reached the kitchen. Nice. Maybe she'd make some cookies, bring them to Darek and Ivy's for Tiger.

She noticed a missed call on the caller ID. Didn't recognize it.

Butter appeared at the back door and Ingrid opened it, then decided to join the dog outside.

The wind cast barren leaves onto the path leading to the dock. The twelve new cabins, winterized and nearly ready for guests, still fragranced the air with the smell of sawdust and fresh paint. Hope for a rebirth of their resort.

So much had burned to ash that day over a year ago when a massive wildfire took out nearly everything they'd built.

Nearly. Sometimes, however, she didn't know how to salvage what they had left.

She followed the dog to the end of the dock, then sat and dangled her bare feet into the water. The wind brushed the trees, a whisper rippling across the lake. The cold nip of waves tugged at her toes. Too soon, the water would sheet over, turn to ice. In their younger years, John would clear a square and they'd spend Sunday afternoons skating. Probably how their children fell in love with hockey.

Butter settled down beside her, sighed deep and long, then put her head in Ingrid's lap. Ingrid ran her hand over Butter's yellow fur. Rubbed under her ear. Butter pressed back, moaning a little with pleasure.

"Yeah, I know, that's what you like. Right there."

Butter lifted her head, her brown eyes meeting Ingrid's. A pained sadness burrowed inside her expression as if to mirror Ingrid's.

Silly tears edged Ingrid's eyes. Oh, good grief. She needed to snap out of this. Despite the recent wounds in her family, everyone would survive. Amelia loved Prague, Eden was living happily ever after in Minneapolis, and Grace was finally reaching for her dreams. Best of all, Darek had made peace with his past, begun a future.

And . . . Casper and Owen would make up. Someday. She had to believe that her family wouldn't stay broken forever.

But she knew, too, that some things could never be fixed.

The dog leaned forward, gave Ingrid's chin a lick.

Ingrid laughed. "I love you too, sweetie." She leaned back on her hands as Butter rolled onto her back. Needing just a bit more love.

Maybe that's all her family needed too, to come back together.

Ingrid rubbed the dog's belly. "Don't you worry, Butter. Everything's going to be fine."

CHAPTER 2

By THE FOURTH QUARTER of the Sunday night game, John had unknotted the problem of the live Nativity and its threat to his Christmas trip.

Darek. John would enlist his eldest son to take over the project. Sure, John would help Ingrid construct the set, but Darek could be there to oversee the event, just as he had the rebuilding of the resort. Together, they'd built twelve sturdy cabins, not to mention resurfaced the basketball court and planted a line of pine trees to cordon off their property from the blackened remains of the forest surrounding it.

Darek was ready to helm the preparations for the grand reopening. And if anyone would understand John's need to take Ingrid away and surprise her, Darek would.

Maybe it would ignite a new flame between himself and Ingrid.

Not that the passion in his marriage had died—it simply needed to be restoked, maybe some new kindling added.

Especially after the cold snap in the car. Yes, of course he'd help her with the setup of the Nativity scene. He just wouldn't stick around for the standing-in-the-cold-for-an-hour part. And he'd have to draw a line in the sand, cut off any hope that he might be willing to play the role of Joseph, the doting husband.

He'd be doting enough in seat 5B, winging their way over the Atlantic to Paris, then Prague.

However, maybe he couldn't wait until Thanksgiving to surprise her with the tickets. Clearly she'd start asking questions—and short of lying to her, John didn't know how to keep her from discovering the secret.

The Steelers kicked off to the Patriots with two minutes remaining, and he decided to tell her on Friday, over dinner. Someplace nice, in town.

Yeah, she'd forget all about their little squabble in the car and the recent chill between them. He'd fix it all by cheering her up, and everything would go back to normal.

No, better than normal.

He turned off the set when the Patriots scored again and headed upstairs. He expected to find lamplight puddling over the bed, Ingrid nose-deep in a novel. But she huddled on the far side of the bed, already sunk into slumber, the room shadowed and nippy.

John climbed into bed, and she stirred as if not quite asleep.

The urge to draw her into his arms swept through him, and he rolled over, intending to rest his hand on her hip.

She emitted a soft snore.

He couldn't wake her. Not when she'd slept so poorly since the family fight this summer. He rolled back, switched off the light.

Friday. He'd fix things on Friday.

He pulled the covers up to his chin, let his brain relax, and imagined Ingrid and him in Paris, on top of the Eiffel Tower. Conjured up her expression as she grinned at him, the sadness vanished, the youth of their romance in her eyes.

"John! Wake up!"

He crawled through the swaddle of sleep and opened his eyes.

Light fell across the comforter, and Ingrid stood above him, wrapped in her pink terry robe. "I need your help."

Huh? He glanced over, just in case he was dreaming, and found her side of the bed empty.

"C'mon, John, please. Help me." She grabbed his arm, and he got up. Outside, the wind howled, rain spitting against the window—a sudden squall. He found his slippers and his robe, pulling them on as he followed Ingrid out of the bedroom.

"What's the matter?" Maybe she wanted him to help close the windows.

"It's Butter. She's sick. She's retching, but nothing's coming up. Her stomach is distended and hard and she's whining. I saw this movie about a dog who had this and died—"

"Honey, I'm sure Butter is fine. She probably ate something in the yard . . ."

Butterscotch lay in the hallway on her side, groaning, her eyes closed. Saliva pooled under her snout on the wood floor.

"She's having trouble breathing," Ingrid said, her voice tight.

John knelt next to the dog, put his hand on her belly. It felt hot, swollen.

Ingrid knelt beside him. "We need to take her to the vet."

"Now? Can't it wait until morning?"

"I don't think so."

He touched her arm. "Honey, Butter will be fine. It's storming outside. We don't want to go out in this—"

"I don't care if it's a category-5 hurricane! Butter needs to go to the vet!" She got up and headed to the bedroom. "If you won't take her, I'll take her by myself."

Oh, for cryin' in the sink—"Okay, just calm down. I'll get dressed." He glanced back at Butter, who opened her eyes and stared at him.

Like he might be the grim reaper.

Nice.

John threw on a pair of jeans, a sweatshirt, socks. Then he went downstairs and pulled on his work boots. Ingrid had already found a stack of old towels. She took them outside, running through the rain to arrange them on the middle seat of her old Caravan.

He put on a rain slicker and tromped back upstairs. "C'mon, let's get you in the car."

The dog tried to bite him as he lifted her into his arms. Figured. "Shh, Butter. It'll be okay."

He held the animal against his chest as Ingrid came back inside. She, too, wore a slicker, the rain dripping from her face, her eyelashes.

She ran her hand over the dog's head as John moved

past her. He dashed out into the night, ducking under the lashing rain, and settled the dog on the middle seat. Butter whined as he shut the door.

Ingrid followed, shoved the keys into his hand, and climbed into the car.

"I already called Kate, and she's meeting us at the clinic."

He didn't want to consider what an emergency visit might cost. Probably the vet would give Butter some fluids and send her home.

As they pulled out, Ingrid turned and put her hand on Butter's head, speaking softly.

"Remember the night when Casper drank that potion Grace and Eden concocted?" John said, more of a murmured memory than a question.

"Yes," Ingrid said quietly. "I still want to kill them for that. Poor kid could never turn down a dare. I thought for sure he had appendicitis."

She glanced up and met John's eyes, a ghost of a smile on her lips. "I'm surprised, frankly, that we didn't have more late-night trips to the ER."

He wanted to reach out then, catch her hand, but she turned back to Butter, speaking comfort to the animal.

John drove to town in silence.

The outside light of the vet's office—more of an attachment to Kate Snyder's home—shone hazy and bright through the rain.

He pulled up near the overhang of the porch, got out, opened the sliding door, then climbed into the Caravan and took Butter into his arms.

Ingrid followed him out, and he spotted Kate outlined in the door of her office. The sound of kenneled dogs— now awake—rose from the back of the building.

Ingrid followed John and Kate into the clinic, and Kate directed them to a room. He passed a very pregnant beagle in a cage, lying on her side. So maybe they hadn't dragged Kate out of bed.

"I found her on my way to the bathroom, collapsed in the hallway, moaning," Ingrid was saying. "She tried to throw up a few times, but nothing came out. And her belly, it's so hard . . ."

John set the dog on the stainless steel table. Butter moaned again as Kate took a stethoscope from the wall. She pulled up Butter's lips, inspecting her gums. She pressed them, watched the blood refill. Even to John's unpracticed eyes, they seemed gray.

Ingrid took off her slicker, hanging it on a hook in the entryway. Apparently they were sticking around. He pulled off his, too, and returned to see Kate starting an IV.

"Can you help her?" Ingrid said.

John put his hand on Ingrid's shoulder. She looked up at him, her eyes wet. Then she leaned against him. He slid his arm around her as she fit into the cradle of his embrace.

"Butter has bloat, and we need to work fast," Kate said. "I need to slow her heart rate down and get some fluids in her, or she'll go into shock. Then I need to get her stomach decompressed."

Ingrid clung to him as Kate worked on Butter. She finished inserting the IV, then turned to John. "I need to put in a stomach tube, and since my assistant is still ten minutes away, I'll need your help, John."

She took a tube from a drawer and ran it from Butter's mouth to her rib cage, marking the distance with a piece of tape. Then she inserted a plastic block with a hole in the center into Butter's mouth, wedging it open, and taped the block in place.

Butter groaned with the ministrations and even more when Kate inserted the lubricated tube into her mouth. Ingrid pressed her hands to her face, and even John gritted his teeth, watching Butter struggle.

But the dog swallowed the tube down. Kate gently slid it into the esophagus, working it into Butter's stomach.

Suddenly gas and fluid began to spill from the tube. Butter whined.

"John, pick up Butter and hold her in a standing position."

He obeyed, and Kate massaged the dog's abdomen to expel the rest of the fluids. Then, finally, she extracted the tube. John put Butter back on the table. The dog closed her eyes, breathing better.

"Is it over?" Ingrid said.

Kate washed her hands in the sink, grabbed a paper towel. "I'm afraid not. That was just to save her life." She threw the towel into the trash. "I need to get X-rays to confirm, but I believe Butter has gastric dilatation, or torsion. It means that her stomach has twisted and she is not able to eat or digest her food. There are toxins in her body as a result of the fermentation in her stomach. It could rupture, or she could even have a heart attack."

Ingrid nodded, her face pale.

Kate sighed. "She'll need surgery, something called gastropexy. It untwists the stomach and tacks it in place."

Surgery. John had already glanced at the fees when hanging up his rain slicker. This visit alone meant he'd have to downgrade their hotel in Paris.

"Could it happen again?" Ingrid asked.

"If she doesn't have the surgery? Yes, and most likely her situation will become graver more quickly."

"She'll die."

"In great pain."

"And if she has the surgery?"

Kate pressed her fingers against Butter's femoral artery, along one of her hind legs. "It could still happen again, although it's much less likely."

Ingrid ran her fingers along her cheek, wiping away the wetness there.

John put his hand on her shoulder, hating the decision they'd have to make. "I'm so sorry, Ingrid." He looked at Kate. "Maybe we should give Tiger a chance to say good-bye—he's awfully attached to Butter. Can you keep her until morning?"

Kate nodded.

"What are you talking about?" Ingrid had rounded on him.

Uh . . . "Don't you think Tiger would want to say good-bye?" He frowned. "Maybe you're right; maybe it'd be too hard for him—"

"Say good-bye? John. Are you seriously suggesting we *put Butter to sleep*?"

The silence in the room turned deadly, and in a second

he realized his folly. He swallowed. Glanced at Butter, eyes closed, miserable on the table. "She's old—"

"She's *family*, John. You don't . . . you don't euthanize your family."

"She's a dog, Ingrid." He reached for her, but she jerked away. He looked at Kate. "How much is the surgery?"

"She'd have to stay for a week at least. . . . Maybe five thousand?"

"Dollars?"

"Well, it's not in pennies, John." Ingrid backed up, her hand on Butter. "But last time I checked our savings, we had that and more. We've got the money—and Butter needs this surgery."

He stood there, trying not to let her words send him reeling, trying not to hear the howl inside. "Ingrid. Be reasonable. It's five thousand dollars. I had plans . . ." He ran his hand behind his neck, turned away. Big plans.

"What plans could possibly be more important than saving Butter's life? A new snowmobile? Maybe repairs on the car?"

"How about a once-in-a-lifetime trip to Europe to see your daughter for Christmas?"

He didn't mean for his words to carry such a sharp edge—didn't mean to say them at all, really. But that's what she did—drove him beyond himself sometimes. Drove him to make decisions out of his control.

Drove him to be the one to face reality.

John took a breath and faced her. He could admit he'd sort of hoped she'd hear his words, let them sink in. In his wildest dreams she actually smiled at him. Agreed.

Not a chance.

Ingrid's mouth was a tight bud of anger. She shook her head. "So this was why you didn't want to do the live Nativity. Because you wanted to spend our savings on a crazy trip to Europe?"

"I thought it would be a nice surprise." He noticed how Kate had grabbed her stethoscope.

"A surprise is flowers, an overnight trip to Minneapolis, even—let's go wild—diamond earrings. A surprise is not stealing me away from my home for Christmas—"

"But no one except Darek and Ivy will be here. And they have their own family now!"

"I'll be here. And Butter—Butter will be here. I know the kids are moving on with their lives and that Christmas won't be the same, but it doesn't mean we have to run away. How do you think Amelia would feel if we showed up in Prague only to tell her that we had to bury Butter?"

A tear dripped off her chin. "Don't you know me at all,

John? I don't want a trip to Europe. I want the dog you gave me to live."

The dog he gave her. In a clarifying moment, he saw it.

He'd brought Butter home just a month after they'd lost their last child to a miscarriage.

He ground his jaw tight and nodded to Kate. "Do whatever you need to do to save Butter's life."

Then he turned, grabbed his slicker, and headed back out to the van, where the rain stirred up the mud and chill of the dark autumn night.

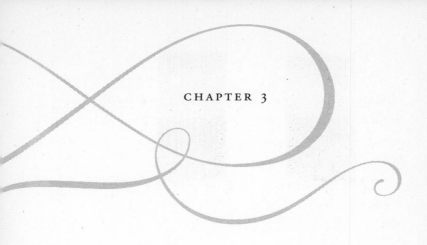

CHAPTER 3

Ingrid added stevia to her pumpkin latte and gave it a stir before meeting Noelle Hueston by the door of the coffee shop. "I can admit it was a sweet gesture. I mean, of course I miss Amelia. And I'd love to see Prague. But Butter is part of the family."

Noelle nodded and held the door open for her. After the rain a week ago, autumn was creeping in more every morning, a sharp chill to the air hinting at the winter hovering just a month or so away. Ingrid had finally scrounged up the enthusiasm to tackle the live Nativity project by rooting out the supplies from community storage. Thankfully, Noelle had shown up to work, her blonde hair tucked under a red bandanna, a vest over her thermal shirt.

"I'm sure John will come around," Noelle said. "Sometimes men simply can't see how to fix something, so they walk away. Like Eli did after Kelsey died. He even packed up all of Kelsey's things as if wiping her out of our lives would make it better."

How Noelle and Eli had managed to put their lives back together after the murder of their daughter still amazed Ingrid.

"How is Butter doing?"

"She's up and around. Recovered from the surgery, although the vet says it'll take a while for her to be fully back to normal."

"And John?"

"Still grieving his trip to Europe." They crossed the street to the old real estate office–turned–community storage, and Noelle dug out the keys, courtesy of her husband, who'd picked them up from Seb Brewster, the mayor.

"Sure, I would love to go," Ingrid continued. "But not right now. What if Casper—and maybe even Owen— wanted to come home for Christmas?"

Noelle eased the door open, and shadows fell over the array of Deep Haven accoutrements: boxes of garland that wound around the light poles along Main Street; the lighted candy canes and wreaths; banners for the annual dragon boat races, Fourth of July, art fair, and Moose Madness festivals; the Christmas lights for the tree in the park. Even the costume for the Deep Haven Huskies mascot had managed to find its way into the assortment.

A cornucopia of hometown pride.

Ingrid shook her head. "I can't believe we're still doing a community live Nativity after all these years."

"I know. But it's part of the landscape of Deep Haven. And besides, this year you, the Christiansens, are heading it up. It's going to be fabulous."

Right. If she and John were still talking to each other by then. They were like the old live Nativity tradition—soldiering on despite a lack of attendance. Ingrid began to search for the costumes, the manger, the lights and props.

"What are the chances of the boys coming home for Christmas?" Noelle asked.

Ingrid unearthed a box marked *Wings*. "Slim. None. Casper e-mailed me a few days ago and said he loved Roatán. He can't leave his work."

"And Owen?"

Ingrid swallowed past the boulder in her throat. Opened the box and found torn and tangled wings. Sighed. "I haven't heard from him since Eden's wedding." She'd hoped he'd rejoined the hotshot firefighting team in Montana, but an e-mail to the head of the team had dispelled that hope.

Noelle had paused in her search. Ingrid looked up.

"I'm sure he's okay," Noelle said softly. "Time heals all wounds."

Really? She didn't want to say it, but she doubted even Noelle believed that. "I know. I just can't get past this idea that we need to do something. I'm still their mother, even if they are adults, and I should help them fix this. But if I interfere, it could make it worse."

"You'll never stop being their mother, but the fact is, you can't pick them up, kiss them, and make it all better anymore."

Ingrid smiled at the image of baby Darek flinging himself into her arms.

Maybe not, but she wanted to. She still had plenty of good mom left in her. She closed up the box. "So I have wings, and there's the manger."

"And I found the Mary and Joseph costumes."

"But where's the set? There should be a barn or something."

Ingrid's phone vibrated in her pocket. She pulled it out and glanced at the number but didn't recognize it. Bracing herself for a telemarketer, she answered.

"Is Ingrid there?" The voice on the other end bore the washboard tones of a lifelong smoker. At first she didn't recognize it, but then . . .

"Kari? Is this you?"

"Hey, Sis."

Hey, Sis. Sixteen years since Ingrid had heard, *Hey, Sis.* Not since the day Kari called looking for a place to land.

The day John had turned her away. Not that Ingrid blamed him, really. But the simplicity, the significance of her greeting rang through time and hollowed Ingrid out. "Are you okay? How did you get this number?" She hadn't exactly meant it to come out angry, but she heard the catch in her sister's voice, so she hurried to add, "It doesn't matter. How are you?"

"I called the house, and Darek answered. He gave it to me." Kari's voice trembled, and Ingrid couldn't bear to imagine where she might be. In a hospital or even in jail, calling for bail money.

No, that thought seemed mean. Probably her sister had happily remarried, finally built a new life for herself and her younger son, Romeo.

She'd heard from her parents that the Army had redeployed Matthew, Kari's older son, for another tour of duty. Maybe . . . "Is Matthew okay?"

"Yeah. He's fine. He's still overseas until Thanksgiving. And that's why I'm calling."

Noelle glanced at Ingrid, then grabbed a box and headed out to the Caravan.

"I need someone to take Romeo until his brother gets home."

"Take Romeo?"

A hiccup of breath, sounding too much like crying. But Ingrid resisted the urge to comfort Kari. Her sister had made a mess of her life, starting with her affair with Romeo's father, which ended her marriage and launched her two children into a life with live-in boyfriends, eviction notices, and welfare.

"I'm going into treatment . . . at least until Christmas, and I have no one to take him."

True. Their mom couldn't handle a sixteen-year-old kid, not with Dad's Alzheimer's creeping up on him. She had her hands full visiting him at the nursing home every day.

"Please, Ingrid. I know we haven't talked for a while—"

"Sixteen years, Kari. You've ignored all my letters."

"I know . . ."

Ingrid was sure there must be a defense hanging off the end of that sentence. But maybe Kari had grown up, because she said nothing.

Or maybe she really did need Ingrid. "Why now? Can't you wait until Matthew gets home?" Not that she didn't want her sister to get help if she needed it, but—"I mean, aren't you living with someone—?"

"It's court ordered. I was arrested and . . . I'm leaving tomorrow. I tried calling you last week, but I couldn't get ahold of you, and then I thought maybe I could put it off, but we lost the request for a delay of sentence, so . . ."

Sentence? Oh, she didn't want to know. "Where are you?"

"Duluth. The social worker said she could bring him tonight. I'll sign papers to make you and John his legal guardians. It's just until Matthew comes home."

Ingrid sighed. Noelle returned for the box of crushed wings.

"Yes, Kari. We'll take Romeo."

"I figured it out." John shot a nail into the two-by-four, securing it to the top plate for the back wall of Darek's house.

Overhead, the blue sky stretched without blemish across the horizon. A slight wind bullied the leaves off the trees and across the decking of Darek's unfinished house.

After living in the lodge following the fire, then in an apartment in town once he and Ivy got married, Darek hoped to have the interior walls finished and the roof shingled by the first snowfall.

"Your mother is afraid of the empty nest." John had taken off his jacket and worked in a thermal shirt and his jeans, a stocking cap over his bald head. Next to him, Darek wore his tool belt, a pair of work jeans, a short-sleeved shirt printed with the words *Jude County Hotshots*.

Darek put down the next board, shoring it up to the pencil mark on the top plate. "I think she just didn't want Butter to die, Dad. I mean, I guess I agree with Mom."

John looked at him.

Darek held up a gloved hand. "Okay, yeah, I see your point. Five grand is a chunk of cash."

"For a dog."

"*Our* dog, Dad. Butterscotch is a part of the family." He held the board in place, picked up the gun.

There were moments when Darek seemed more like a friend than his eldest son, and John sometimes caught himself talking out of turn.

But certainly Darek would understand this. "I know she is. And I didn't know how much until I realized that Butter, in a way, took the place of Benjamin."

Darek glanced up, catching him with his blue eyes, so much like Ingrid's. He frowned under his gimme cap.

"Your little brother."

"Yeah, I remember." Darek went back to his work. "It's just, we don't talk about him."

"I always thought it might be too difficult for your mom. She took it hard."

"I did too. We thought we'd have a little brother for Christmas."

Christmas. Yeah, he'd forgotten that Benjamin had been due in late November.

"We got Butter instead." Darek nailed the board into place. "You got that bottom plate?"

John picked up the two-by-six and began to nail it across the bottom of the wall. "Getting your mother a dog to ease her pain after the miscarriage probably wasn't the brightest gift, but I didn't know what else to do."

"I think it was the perfect gift, Dad." Darek kicked some of the wallboards into place, held them as his dad nailed them. "Except, can I ask why you and Mom never had another child?"

The question stirred up the memory, the swift rush of pain to his chest. "I nearly lost your mother, too, that day. I decided that six kids were enough."

Darek went silent. Then, "With nearly losing Butter, maybe Mom is reliving all that pain again."

Since when had Darek gotten so insightful? "You sound like an old married man."

Darek laughed. "I am. And . . . I'm going to be a dad again."

John looked at him, and Darek grinned. Nodded.

"Really. When?"

"Sometime this spring. Ivy just found out this week. Don't tell Mom yet—we're going to surprise her at Christmas."

"I'm not sure you should wait that long."

"Ivy's idea. She wants to give Mom a picture of the ultrasound for Christmas."

"Another good reason why leaving for Christmas wasn't my best idea." John finished nailing the bottom plate and set down the gun. "But I have to admit: I never thought it would land me in the doghouse."

"It's not the trip, Dad. Mom's upset about Owen and Casper. And the fact that they're fighting. And maybe, yeah, this Butter thing has stirred up the past. Maybe she's just seeing an end too soon to her mothering." He positioned himself on the far end of the wall, next to John.

"I thought she'd be thrilled to have the house to ourselves. You know, with Naked Tuesday and everything."

Darek looked at him, appalled. "Really? You had to say that?"

John grinned.

Darek shook his head. "Pick up that end and start acting like my father."

John laughed. "On the count of three."

Darek counted and they lifted the wall together, moving it into place. John held it as Darek tacked in the wall braces.

"I just want to help her realize that there's so much more ahead of us. Vacations and new hobbies, and maybe she'll even get me to take dance lessons."

"Who are you, and what have you done with my stick-in-the-mud father?" Darek finished tacking the last board. He walked over to the framed-in windowsill and grabbed a Coke.

John chuckled. "So maybe dance lessons are a little overboard. But that's the point—if we want to take dance lessons, now we can. And your mom needs to see that."

"And you're going to prove it to her."

"Just because we can't go to Europe doesn't mean we can't—"

"If you say 'have Naked Tuesdays,' I'm throwing my hammer at you."

"Have fun. Be young again. Do those carefree things we used to do before you came along."

"Blame it all on me, huh?"

John sat down on the steps, staring out at the lake. "Once upon a time, we'd spend afternoons swimming in this lake or hiking up to Honeymoon Bluff or lying under the sky, debating cloud shapes. I miss that. It feels like it's been a while since I heard her laugh."

Behind him, Darek said nothing. John finally turned, and Darek gave him a long, enigmatic look, then sighed.

"What?"

"Mom laughs, Dad. She laughs with Tiger and Ivy."

But she didn't laugh with her husband—not anymore—and that realization stung as it filtered inside. Worse, he couldn't pinpoint when she had stopped.

The wind scattered leaves in the dirt yard and tumbled a Coke can from the steps. John ran after it, catching it. Somehow, he needed to figure out how to make his wife laugh again.

"I gotta knock off. Ivy's going to the doctor today, and I have to pick up Tiger from school." Darek took off his tool belt. "I'll be here tomorrow morning. However, I won't stop by the house, since it's Tuesday."

John grinned at him, and Darek winked, headed out to

his truck. John watched his broad-shouldered son saunter away. *I'm going to be a dad again.*

Yeah, those had been good years. But maybe he didn't have to wait for a trip to Europe—or a special occasion—to reignite his marriage.

Maybe he could do it today, right now. On a Monday afternoon.

He put a cover over the table saw, tarped the other tools, then headed to the lodge.

"Ingrid?"

He heard her humming upstairs. Untying his boots, he left them in the entryway and found her in the boys' bedroom, remaking Owen's bed.

He couldn't deny the spark inside. "Is Owen coming home?"

Ingrid wore a Deep Haven Huskies T-shirt and a pair of jeans, her blonde hair pulled back in a blue bandanna. She looked over her shoulder at him, then shook her head. She finished pulling up the quilt, turned to the bureau, and opened the top drawer. "He hasn't lived here in three years, and still, he leaves his dirty socks in his drawers." She scooped them out and dropped them into a clothes basket.

"What are you doing?"

"I'm making room." She closed the bureau drawer.

"For . . . ?"

Ingrid sighed, then picked up the clothes basket, propping it on her hip, almost like a shield between them. "For Romeo."

He had nothing.

"Romeo? My sister's kid?"

And it started to click. Romeo, the kid Kari had with the guy she left her husband for. Or something like that.

He did, however, clearly remember the phone call when she'd asked to move to Deep Haven. To the resort. To hide and perhaps dump all her problems on them. He gave Ingrid a grim look. "Ingrid—"

"She's going into treatment, John, and Romeo needs a place to stay."

"How old is he—twelve?"

"Sixteen. Wow." She moved past him. Like . . . that was the end of the conversation?

"So she's not coming with him? Are you sure?"

Ingrid rounded on him. "For a guy who had a crush on my sister, you sure have turned on her."

"She's a mess, and she brings her mess with her. I just don't want—"

"Her mess? Her emotional issues?"

"She's a disaster, and we just got our lives back."

She frowned at him, and he realized that hadn't come out right. As usual.

"I didn't realize they were taken from us."

"Ingrid, I didn't mean it like that. It's just . . . with the kids gone, we have a chance to really have fun, you know? Take vacations—"

"I don't want to go to Europe."

"Okay, so maybe Florida or California."

She shook her head and left the room.

Sorry, but he wasn't giving up that easily. "Or maybe we start doing something fun like . . . like . . . dance lessons!"

Even to his own ears, he sounded desperate, but it stopped her and she turned, staring at him. "Seriously? Dance lessons? That's what you want?"

No. He wanted . . . he wanted . . . He couldn't put it into words maybe, but he wanted what he'd always thought they had but couldn't exactly enjoy because, well, life took over. Kids and mortgage and running the resort.

He wanted to hear her laugh and to know he'd made that happen.

"Romeo needs a place to stay. It's only until Thanksgiving. And then don't worry; it'll just be you and me and this big empty house. All your dreams come true."

John swallowed hard, feeling her words in his chest.

And Butter. He wasn't sure where that came from, and he knew it would only make it worse to say it, but, "Don't forget; we still have Butter."

She sighed, her face softening. "Yes. We still have Butter."

The words hung between them, a quiet epitaph on their lives.

The sound of the doorbell shook them free. Ingrid met his eyes. "Try to remember that the sins of his mother are not his. He just needs a little love."

John bit back the words, but he had to wonder if Romeo was perhaps coming to the wrong house.

CHAPTER 4

ROMEO SHOVED spoonfuls of macaroni and cheese into his mouth like a starving man.

"Would you like more?" Ingrid said, reaching for his nearly empty plate.

He glanced at her, nodded. "Thanks, Aunt Ingrid."

That sounded weird. But what else was he supposed to call her? Mom? He did remind her, in a way, of her sons. Although taller than her boys, he had their athletic build. Wide shoulders; lean, strong frame. He wore a thin black Nike sweatshirt over loose-fitting jeans, and she recognized in his face traces of her beautiful sister—the high cheekbones, the dark-blond hair, the green eyes. The look of nonchalance. Like nothing mattered—he could shrug off the world or own it with a smile.

She doubted she'd see any hint of a smile soon, however. He'd arrived glum and uncaring as the social worker showed them where to sign the legal custody papers, then notarized them. "It's just a short-term guardianship," she'd explained. "You can transfer it when Matthew gets back from his deployment."

"Or I turn seventeen and join the military," Romeo said as he dumped his backpack and floppy green duffel bag in the hallway. Ingrid had frowned at the social worker.

"He wants to be an emancipated minor," the woman said. "But he needs a guardian's signature." She handed Ingrid a sheaf of papers. "His school transcripts, medical records, and other pertinent information. His mother will be at a treatment center just north of Duluth. She has no visitation until Thanksgiving, so I'll be in touch."

Ingrid nodded, and the woman pressed a card into her hand. Then she said good-bye to Romeo, who'd already found a place on a stool at the counter, thumbing his iPhone. Unaffected.

Until Ingrid put a plate of homemade macaroni and cheese in front of him.

He looked up. "Not out of a box?"

"Nothing out of a box here, kiddo," she had said and then wondered if that might be too friendly. But maybe that's what her nephew—that felt weird to call this stranger—needed.

Now she refilled his plate, then turned to pull a sheet of fresh-baked cookies from the oven. Across the room, John turned a page in his newspaper. He'd lit a fire, and it crackled in the hearth. Butter lay on the floor, still lethargic from surgery, but improving every day. Soon she'd be well enough to go for a walk.

We still have Butter.

She wasn't sure what John had meant by that . . . but the words hung in her mind.

She scooped the cookies off the tray and set them on a wooden sheet to cool. Putting three on a plate, she brought them to John.

A peace offering.

He took the plate, smiled at her. "Thanks, honey."

She nodded and returned to the kitchen. "Cookies?" she asked Romeo.

"Thank you." He reached for them and then the glass of milk she poured. As he bent over the cup, dunking the cookies, it stirred up a memory of Darek or perhaps Casper doing the same—hair falling over his eyes, milk dripping from his chin.

Or maybe the memory she conjured resembled John,

during those early days of their newlywed year when he'd arrive home to fresh-baked cookies.

Ingrid glanced at John. He'd finished off the cookies. She should have brought him milk.

Next time.

She leaned against the counter. "So tomorrow we'll enroll you at the high school. You're a junior, right?"

Romeo nodded, dunking his cookie, letting the milk stream off it. "I think so. I missed a little school when we moved to Chicago, but I made it up in summer school, in Memphis, so I think I'm caught up."

Chicago? Memphis? "How many places have you lived, Romeo?" She scooted two more cookies onto his plate. He didn't hesitate.

He had strong hands and forearms, like he lifted weights. Maybe he played a sport. She could imagine him in hockey pads, his blond hair curling out from under a helmet.

"Um . . . I dunno. A lot." He lifted a shoulder.

His answer felt awkward, as if it should be something she knew. "I'm sorry about your mom. I'm sure she'll be fine."

Again the shoulder shrug, but his mouth tightened around the edges.

"Do you talk to your brother much?"

He shook his head. "I have his e-mail address, though."

John glanced at her, then back at the paper and turned the page.

"We'll e-mail him, let him know you're all right."

Romeo said nothing.

"I put you up in the boys' room, first door on the left. You can unpack your clothes into the empty dresser in the window alcove."

He got up, brought his plates to the sink, and rinsed them.

Huh.

"Thank you," he said quietly.

"No problem. If you tell me what you like to eat, I can try to make it for you."

He frowned at her. "I'll eat anything."

Oh.

He headed to the entry to retrieve his duffel bag and backpack, so she opened a can of dog food and filled Butter's dish. Setting it on the floor, she called the dog.

Butter got off the floor and plodded to the bowl, groaning softly as she walked.

"What's wrong with her?" Romeo stood with his duffel over his shoulder.

"She had surgery a few days ago. She's still recovering. She just needs a little TLC."

He stood there a moment, something in his eyes. "I had a dog once. It was a rescue dog that my da—that Eddie had. He was a hound dog, I think. Loved to chase cars."

He hitched the strap up on his shoulder and turned to take the stairs.

"What happened to him?"

He stopped on the first step. Shrugged again. "He got sick and died."

"I'm so sorry," Ingrid said. "It's so horrible to lose a pet."

Romeo gave a small grunt. "Yeah, I guess. I was talking about Eddie. The dog ran away."

He trudged up the stairs, disappearing at the top.

Only then did Ingrid realize she'd caught her breath and couldn't move.

She heard John, behind her, close the paper. "I know what you're thinking, Ingrid. You can't fix this kid. He's as much of a mess as his mother."

She didn't look at him as she headed for the stairs. "That's where you're wrong, John. He just needs a little TLC."

"In two short weeks, we've reverted back to the high school years." John kept up with Nate, breathing hard, the crisp air cooling his body as they ran Pincushion Trail, overlooking Deep Haven. "Every day, she picks up Romeo from school, comes home, and serves us dinner, like he's our kid or something. She even prints out his homework assignments from the school and checks his papers."

"It's in her blood, John. Ingrid can't help but be a mom." Nate slowed as they reached the overlook. The array of full-on autumn could steal John's breath if he looked at it with a fresh eye. Gold, crimson, pine green, and browns patchworked the hillside that cascaded toward town.

"She's bonding with this kid, and when his brother shows up to take him, she'll be brokenhearted." He leaned over, gripped his knees.

"And what do you think of him?" Nate leaned against a sign, beginning to stretch out his calves. A wind snaked through the trees, tugging at John's sweatshirt, tossing leaves across the path, the smell of winter on the traces.

"He's okay. Quiet. I don't know. Maybe not as much trouble as I thought he'd be. Polite, even." John straightened and scanned the blue of the lake, spotting a tanker miles offshore.

"He sounds like a good kid."

"Who's going to break Ingrid's heart. And frankly she's had enough of that with Casper and Owen."

"No word from Owen?"

John shook his head. But he refused to worry. Leave that to Ingrid.

They turned and started down the path to their cars. "So how's the live Nativity coming along?" Nate said.

"Ingrid has boxes of broken wings and ratty costumes all over the living room. The manger looks as if a horde of kids stomped on it, and we're still trying to find the stable. Apparently the Congregational Church lost track of it last year."

"I know that they got a few bunnies last year from the Bergstroms for the petting zoo. And you might check with the Westerlinds for goats."

"I'll tell Ingrid." He followed Nate into the parking lot, where his truck sat in the late-afternoon sunshine.

Nate stretched out against the hood of his sedan. "You know, it sounds like this kid has had a rough go of it. You might consider that you're one of the few father figures he's ever had."

John pulled off his sweatshirt, tossed it into the cab. "I'm not his father. And I don't want to be. I did that, and I'm done."

Nate nodded. "Yeah. I get that. See you at church." He got into his car, waving as he pulled away.

John picked up his phone as he slid onto the bench seat. A text message from Ingrid was displayed on the screen. **Please pick up Romeo from the school.**

He checked his watch. The kid would be outside, getting into who knows what kind of trouble by now. He backed out and headed to the school, pulling up in the parking lot.

He spied a couple of kids sitting on a picnic table near the door, but no Romeo. He hoped the kid wasn't somewhere living up to his name. John had no doubt that with his new-kid reputation and his golden locks, Romeo had a flock of girls following him through the halls.

He sat for a moment, then shoved the truck into park and got out, heading inside.

Although locked during the day, the school opened after hours for parents picking up kids. He heard voices from the weight room and ducked his head in, the smells of sweaty athletic gear rousing old memories. He half expected to see Darek or Casper grinning at him from the bench press. Or even Nate at the squatting bar, back in the days when they ran the school.

"Anyone seen Romeo?" He felt strange just asking that. Who named their child Romeo? Poor guy. For a second, John considered that such a name might brand the kid. Force a chip on his shoulder.

Maybe he needed to give Romeo kudos if he didn't find him wrapped up like a pretzel in some girl's arms.

He walked through the school, checked the gym, a few of the rooms, and finally found himself out back. The football team was scrimmaging on the practice field and the shrill of the whistle stirred up the past. John could see the crowd rising to their feet as he ran onto the field, a fleeting thrill before he sank into the game. He could smell the excitement in the air, taste the fear of the other team, feel the adrenaline as he leveled someone.

Football had helped him understand what it meant to be a man. Hard work, focus. He'd tried not to let it bother him that none of his boys played, that he spent Sundays alone in his recliner, watching the Vikings.

Maybe Benjamin would have been the football player in the family. He'd never considered that.

In fact, he hadn't spent much time at all thinking of the son they'd lost. Life simply drove over him then, with the responsibilities of taking care of six kids, running the resort, trying to figure out what to do with his relief.

He'd never spoken the words aloud, but in truth, he'd feared adding another mouth to the family. Had tried to drum up enthusiasm for this surprise baby and failed.

He'd betrayed Ingrid in that; he knew it.

The sounds of practice drew him onto the field. He watched a few sets and, despite himself, made some mental notes. The defensive end had to close that gap or the running back would drive a semi through it.

"John, are you here to check out our new recruit? It's about time we saw a Christiansen kid on the field." Seb Brewster, mayor and assistant coach, came over to him. A big man who'd played college ball, Seb still looked like he could dodge defenders and land the pigskin between the yellow markers. He wore a Deep Haven Huskies T-shirt, his biceps stretching the fabric. Out on the field, Caleb Knight, head coach, brought the team in with a whistle.

John met Seb's outstretched hand. "What are you talking about?"

Seb frowned, turned toward the field. Pointed. "Number 63. He's yours, right? Romeo?"

John stared at the kid, now removing his helmet to take a knee and listen to the coach. Long blond hair caught in the wind. "Well, he's my wife's sister's kid, but . . . for now, I guess so."

"He's catching on fast. It's a little late in the season, but he's still eligible, so if he keeps digging in, he might see some playing time."

"Is he playing end?"

"Yeah, strong side."

"He's not holding his ground. He's got to learn to turn the runner inside. Let the outside linebacker pick him off."

"He could use some backyard coaching, for sure. But he's got heart."

On the field, the coach drew the kids in, hands in the middle. They chanted, broke free, and ran to the sidelines.

Romeo slowed as he saw John. His hair hung in sweaty strings around his head, his practice jersey grimy and sodden. Hard work, focus. He saw it in the kid's demeanor.

John lifted his chin in acknowledgment. "I'll be in the truck."

Wandering back through the school, he stopped at the trophy case. Spied his own grinning mug in the state championship photo.

He pulled his sweatshirt on when he got into the truck, checked his phone, and texted Ingrid that he'd found Romeo.

Why hadn't she told him about Romeo going out for football?

Romeo climbed in beside him, tossing his backpack on the seat. "Sorry I'm late. Practice went over."

John glanced at the kid as he reached for his buckle. He'd showered, his hair still wet on his shirt, looking like he'd hurried from the locker room. He was shivering in the cool evening.

Aw, shoot. "Listen. You gotta get more aggressive. You got a regular six-lane highway out there right now. Stand your ground."

Romeo eyed him, and John braced himself.

Then, "How?"

How. He hadn't expected that. But seeing Romeo stare at him, big eyes, John had the crazy urge to get out on the grass with him. Play a little two-handed touch football. He shook away the feeling. "How? You get low and attack the outside shoulder of the defender with your inside shoulder. You'll push him where you want him and then be free to attack the runner."

Romeo nodded, and John turned away, putting the truck into gear.

Romeo rode in silence. Finally he said, "Thank you, Mr. Christiansen."

John reached for the heater, switched it on. "I'm your uncle John. And you're in luck because I think your aunt is making pot roast for supper."

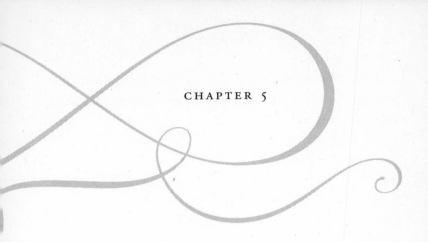

CHAPTER 5

INGRID EASED OPEN THE DOOR and walked into the bedroom.

"Here's the deal, Romeo. I'm not just a mom; I'm a *sports* mom, so I know when an athlete is hiding pain."

Romeo sat on the floor in his sweatpants and T-shirt, stretching his legs, his face in a grimace. "I'm a little tight, is all."

"Heads up." She tossed him an ice pack. "Try that on your calf. It will help with the tension and loosen it up."

He gave her a half smile. "How'd you know?"

"You were limping after dinner."

He wrapped the pack around his leg. "I'm just sore. I'll be good for Friday's game."

He didn't ask her if she'd be attending, but she heard

it in the silence. She came closer, pulled the quilt off the bed, and hooked him around one shoulder to help ease him up. "My boys played hockey, not football, but your uncle John used to play."

Romeo settled back into the pillows. "For the Minnesota Gophers. I saw his picture in the hallway."

She picked up his socks, tossed them into the basket in the closet. "Defensive end. I even caught one of his games."

"Only one?"

"We weren't dating until after college. But I still wanted to see him play." Sitting at the end of his bed, she smoothed the quilt. "I had a terrible crush on him for years before he noticed me." In fact, it sometimes felt as though she'd loved him her entire life. She'd forgotten that feeling lately. But seeing Romeo in his T-shirt, icing his leg, flashed a memory of John on crutches. Wide-shouldered, long hair, he'd looked broken then, as if he needed her, and she loved him even more.

"He actually injured his knee his freshman year and had to work his way back onto the team. I've never seen anyone with as much sheer toughness as your uncle John."

"How come your kids didn't play football?"

"I don't know. Darek started playing hockey when he was about six years old and loved it. We wanted to let our kids choose their own sports, so we dove in. But I think John always wished he'd had a son who played football." She refused to let her thoughts land there. "Did you play for your last school?"

He nodded. "It seems to be the only thing I'm good at."

She doubted that. "I'll bet your mom enjoys coming to your games."

He shook his head. "She's never been. Working or something. I don't know. But maybe someday. Next year . . ." He looked at her then, his eyes finding hers. "Why didn't we ever . . . ? I mean, how come Mom never talks about you?"

Butter nudged the door open and padded into the room. Ingrid ran her hand over the dog's body as she plopped down on the floor next to the bed. "Your mom and Uncle John had a terrible fight right after you were born. She wanted to move here, but . . . well, it was a difficult time for us, and Uncle John thought he was protecting me. So he told her no. She got angry and, despite the letters I sent to her, refused to forgive."

"She told me that you said she was a horrible mother."

Ingrid frowned and shook her head. "I never said that."

He looked away then. "I don't think she ever really wanted me."

"Romeo, that's not true. She loves you—"

"No. If you love someone, you don't act like they annoy you. You like them, and you try to make them think they're the most important person in the world to you. And you never, ever push them away, make them leave you."

She stared at him, his words thickening her throat. She swallowed hard. Softened her voice. "She didn't have a choice, Romeo. And this is not forever. You'll be back with your mom by Christmas."

He shrugged.

She got up, fighting the overwhelming urge to kiss him on the forehead. But he didn't belong to her.

"Why does Butter come in here every night?" He dropped his hand down, running his fingers through the dog's fur.

"Because you're in Owen's bed, and she loves Owen the best."

"Maybe she loves me the best now."

Ingrid smiled at that. "Probably."

John was already in bed watching the Food Network when she came in. "Hey," he said.

She went to the bathroom, changed into her pajamas, and came out.

He turned off the television. "Why didn't you tell me that Romeo went out for football?"

She smoothed lotion on her face, sitting at the edge of the bed, her back to him. "I didn't think you cared."

"Well . . . I . . . I mean . . . of course I care."

"Really? Because you barely talk to Romeo."

"I talk to him."

She didn't answer, reaching for more lotion.

"Ingrid—I talk to him."

"Mmm-hmm."

"Okay. How about this? We'll go to the game on Friday night."

"I think that would be nice." She climbed under the covers, pulled them up to her chin.

"He reminds me . . . of me."

She didn't expect that—or the strange tone to his voice. She opened her eyes and found him staring straight ahead. "Oh?"

"I was just thinking . . . I don't know. About the boys, I guess. And how none of them played football."

"No, they didn't, did they?"

"They might have, if I'd tried harder to get them to love it."

"I don't know, John. It feels like either you're born with it or you aren't. Our boys love hockey. It's sort of like football, except on skates."

He frowned at her. "It's nothing like football."

"There's pads and helmets."

"And a puck and sticks . . ." He shook his head. Leaned back against the headboard. "Seb says that he's good. Tough."

She closed her eyes. "Of course he is. With a name like Romeo, he'd have to be."

"Yeah, he would. Maybe that's why your crazy sister named him that. Because she knew he'd never have a dad, and he'd have to be tough."

Opening her eyes again, she looked at him. "He could have a dad. At least a sort of dad, if—"

His quick glance cut her off. "I'm not his dad, Ingrid. I'm his uncle. I have my own sons, and I don't want any more."

She drew in a breath. Of course not.

"Good night, John," she said and rolled over.

Just because he didn't want to be Romeo's father—or a father figure—didn't mean that John didn't care about the kid. Or want to cheer him on.

"John, over here!" Nate waved his hand from the middle of the bleachers, where he and Annalise had set up camp. They sat on padded stadium seats, dressed in parkas and blue-and-white Huskies-emblazoned caps, a blanket over their laps. Annalise sported a pom-pom that she raised and shook as the band warmed up with the Deep Haven High fight song.

John glanced behind him at Ingrid, who carried a blanket. They'd left their stadium chairs at home. "Want me to run home and get our seats?"

"Don't be silly. We have five minutes until kickoff. I'll be fine." She smiled past him, toward their friends, and climbed the stairs. John followed, glancing at the field, at the players warming up, running in place, dropping to the grass for push-ups, standing for jumping jacks. Calisthenics designed to intimidate the other team.

He could admit he missed it, and suddenly the long-dormant desire to see one of his boys on the field filled his chest.

Darek would have made a fabulous defensive end.

He scanned the field as he slid into the row behind Ingrid, looking for Romeo. Finally he spotted him running to the bench with the team, fist high.

"It's about time you attended a game," Nate said as the fans took to their feet. "Although I half expected to see you on the field. Feels like yesterday I was sitting up here with the band, watching you blitz the quarterback."

John laughed, caught Ingrid smiling up at him, and a strange heat tunneled through him. She looked pretty tonight in her white snowball cap, blue mittens, a Deep Haven High sweatshirt layered over a fleece jacket. The stars winked down at them from a Husky-blue sky, and in the distance, the moon lasered a path across the big lake. "I've never noticed the view before," he said.

"It's one of the perks of sitting in the bleachers in thirty-six degrees," Annalise said. "We started attending when Jason was in the band. Now we're addicted to small-town football."

The announcer introduced the team, and John ignored the strange pinch of disappointment when Romeo's name wasn't in the starting lineup. But when he ran out for kick-off, John watched him all the way down the field.

He got hit hard but stayed on his feet long enough to add to the pile bringing down the returner.

Ingrid glanced at him. "That was pretty good, right?"

He lifted a shoulder.

The Huskies were playing the Barnett Eagles and by halftime were up by six, Romeo on the field for three kickoff returns. John bounced to his feet twice, shouting when the defensive line let a runner score around the outside.

"You want to go down there?" Ingrid said at halftime, winking.

"Maybe."

"Just a guess, but I don't think the pads will fit you anymore." She grinned at him, and again, that almost-unfamiliar heat twined through him.

She pulled a thermos from her bag and opened the lid. "Cocoa?"

He'd forgotten about the picnics they used to have in the stands at hockey games—hot cocoa, popcorn, sometimes sandwiches. She'd reverted right back into her sports-mom persona.

"No thanks," he said. Maybe this was a bad idea, attending this game, stirring up the sense that they might be a family of sorts. Romeo was just a lodger—and as long as Ingrid remembered that, no one would get hurt.

"Ingrid, do you need help sewing any costumes for the live Nativity?" Ellie Matthews trekked down to their row. "And Dan wanted to know if you wanted the hospitality committee to organize hot cocoa in the fellowship hall afterwards."

"That would be perfect, Ellie, thanks. I found the box of wings, and they need to be repaired. I think if we can get parents to donate sheets, we can create a nice chorus of angels with the children's Sunday school classes."

"I'll talk to the Sunday school superintendent, see if we can make that happen. Have you decided on a Mary and Joseph yet?"

"Nope. But don't worry; I have a few ideas in mind." Ingrid turned back to the game as Ellie left. "I wonder if Romeo would be willing to help. You know, be a shepherd or something."

John looked at her. "Romeo will be gone by Christmas. You know that, right?"

She didn't look at him, wrapping her hands around her cup. "Mmm-hmm."

"Ingrid—the second his brother arrives in the States, Romeo's going to live with him. Right?"

She still didn't look at him. "Yeah. Of course." She blew on the cocoa. "You sure you don't want some of this? It's homemade."

He pursed his lips. "I'm sure."

Overhead, a few clouds had moved in, blotting out the stars. A wind picked up, and as the team came out for the second half, the temperature dropped. His gaze went—too often—to Romeo on the sideline, stamping his feet to keep warm.

The Eagles scored on the kickoff, tying, then leading by one point.

John couldn't help but coach in his head as he watched the sophomore defensive end—the starter—get mowed over, again and again.

Close the gap, turn him to the inside—

And then it happened. The defensive end came off the line hard, got hit, went down, and another player landed on him.

As the play cleared, screams echoed off the field, and the stands hushed to a horrified silence.

Coach Knight ran onto the field as Seb motioned for the ambulance. John gritted his teeth, claws in his gut as he watched them carry the kid off, his leg splinted.

Ingrid held Annalise's hand, watching the spectacle with wide eyes. John rested a hand on her shoulder.

Almost in slow motion, he saw Coach Knight turn, searching, gesturing—and Romeo took the field, strapping on his helmet.

In a strange way, John took the field with him. He lined up beside him, or behind him, coaching him into the play. Felt the hits, winced when he got flattened, cheered when he swept his defender and blitzed the quarterback. Found his feet when Romeo caused a fumble.

And watched with an eerie, almost-painful sense of pride as Romeo did everything John had told him to do and shut down the running play on that side of the field.

The Huskies punched it into the goal one more time for the win, and when the whistle blew, John began to breathe.

"Good game!" Nate high-fived him. "And if I didn't know he wasn't your son, I would guess Romeo is from Christiansen blood."

John had nothing for that—and he couldn't look at Ingrid. Not when she'd been right.

Shoot, but he liked this kid. And if he didn't watch himself, Ingrid wouldn't be the only one getting hurt when Romeo left.

As they headed out of the stands, the sky began to sift out glistening snowflakes across the lights, landing like fairy dust on the field.

CHAPTER 6

A LAYER OF CRISPY SNOW coated her yard, concealing the blemishes that remained from the forest fire over a year ago. Ingrid stood at the window a moment, watching the waves against the shore, the bushy pine trees, a golden sun melting away the clouds.

How quickly the seasons had changed, grace blanketing her world, a dusting of the magic to come.

"Nana!"

The voice turned her, and she set down her hot cocoa just in time for Tiger to leap into her arms. "Oh, you're getting so big!"

"I made this in church today!" He handed her a turkey, made from the outline of his hand, cut, colored, and glued to a Popsicle stick.

"Apparently we're supposed to post it on our fridge for the month as a reminder to be thankful," Ivy said, setting a towel-wrapped casserole on the counter.

"I agree," Ingrid said. "I'm thankful for my family. And especially for nose kisses." She rubbed her nose against Tiger's and he giggled. Then he scampered over to Butter, launching himself at the dog, playing with her ears.

Butter opened an eye, bored, but lifted her head to lick him.

They'd made the right decision about her surgery, even if it had cost their savings. And the trip to Europe. And perhaps even a smidge of warmth between her and John. Although maybe he'd finally forgiven her.

At least a little.

He'd seemed less annoyed with her, perhaps, in the two weeks since they'd attended Romeo's game. Maybe it had everything to do with Romeo and the fact that he loved football as much as John did.

Or maybe John simply realized how well Romeo fit into their family. Easily, as if he'd always belonged here. Like when he'd helped Ingrid take Butter to the vet for a checkup, carrying the dog to the car without being asked and then soothing her on the table.

And Ingrid couldn't deny the turn of her motherly

heart watching him play with a litter of puppies tumbling over one another in a gated area of the foyer. He'd made friends with the runt and returned home with puppy kisses on his chin.

Yeah, Romeo fit, and today, right now, she intended to soak in the joy of having her family around the table for Sunday dinner, without a football game to interfere.

Until the 7 p.m. Vikings kickoff against the Lions.

"What did you bring?" she asked Ivy as she unwrapped the towel.

"Apple crisp," Ivy said, pulling out plates. "The lasagna smells amazing."

"Hey, Dad," Darek said, settling down on the sofa and grabbing the sports section.

John leaned back in his recliner, paging through the editorials. "Son."

Romeo came down the stairs, having changed after church into a pair of sweatpants and a Huskies sweatshirt Ingrid had purchased from the booster club. He'd given her not even a mumble of complaint when she woke him for church that first Sunday or in the weeks since. But although he sat quietly in the pew as if listening, she noticed he didn't sing along, didn't crack the pew Bible.

At least he attended.

He came over, took the plates from Ivy. Brought them to the table.

Ivy glanced at Ingrid, wearing an expression of approval. But that was Romeo—a charmer to the bone. Ingrid had figured that out about two days into his stay, and he hadn't broken her heart yet.

He returned for glasses while Ivy tossed the salad. Ingrid pulled the lasagna from the oven, then the garlic bread wrapped in foil.

"Smells good, Mom." Darek got up, taking the casserole pan to the table. "I can't remember the last time we had lasagna."

"It's Romeo's favorite."

Romeo glanced at her, wearing a hint of a smile. "How did you—?"

"You told me about that time you visited Grandma and Grandpa Young on your birthday and they served you lasagna. This is my mother's recipe."

He gave her a full grin now, and she could feast on it.

She put the garlic bread on the table and surveyed it. "Water—"

"I'm on it," Romeo said, grabbing a pitcher from the cupboard.

John came to the table. "Tiger, it's time to eat. Go wash your hands."

Tiger gave Butter a kiss on her head, then ran to the bathroom, emerging a moment later with the front of his shirt sopping wet.

Ingrid hid a smile as Ivy dried him off, then scooted him onto his chair. Romeo sat next to him. "Hey, kid."

He held up his fist, and Tiger bumped it, saying, "Pow!" Apparently they'd developed a ritual.

John watched, wearing a frown.

Ingrid held out her hands. "Let's pray."

And for a moment, as John's voice rose, all felt right. As it should be. Her family around her, safe. Whole.

"Amen," John said.

Indeed.

They dug into the meal and Ingrid dished up extra for Romeo. He grinned at her.

"So you started in Friday's away game, huh?" Darek passed him the salad.

"Yeah. Rigley is out, so they put me in."

"What was it that they were calling you before the game?" Romeo made a face. "Chunks."

Ingrid raised an eyebrow.

"Because I sorta lose it before every game."

"Ew," Ivy said. "I suddenly don't feel well."

Darek turned to her, concern on his face. "Are you sick?"

She laughed. "I'm just kidding, Darek. Stop worrying."

Why would Darek worry? The question landed on Ingrid's lips just as John reached for the bread and said, "If you keep playing like this, you'll wind up in the play-offs."

"Yeah. I guess."

"Maybe your brother will make it back in time to see a game."

Romeo set his fork down and reached for his glass of milk. "Yeah. Maybe." He took a drink.

Ingrid wanted to turn her husband to ash. "You know what you should do after lunch? Take Tiger outside and play some football. See if Darek and Tiger can keep up with you and Romeo."

Now John was frowning at her.

Romeo looked at her, then at John. Swallowed. "That sounds fun."

"Yeah! And Butter can play too!" Tiger waved his fork in the air as if in triumph. Ivy grabbed for his wrist before he cast tomato sauce onto the walls.

John nodded. "Sure."

"I'll help work on the costumes for the live Nativity," Ivy said. "I can glue wings."

"What is a live Nativity, anyway?" Romeo said.

"It's a community project. Every year, one church hosts the Christmas Eve live Nativity scene, complete with a small petting zoo for the kids—goats, bunnies, sheep, and a live Mary and Joseph. The kids dress up as angels and shepherds, and the community gathers to sing carols together. It's really quite festive. I signed us up a couple years ago and then forgot about it."

"Sounds . . ."

"Cold?" John said. "Yes, it is. Mary and Joseph have to stand there for at least an hour while the community sings songs and the pastor of the church gives a sermonette."

"When did you become the Grinch, Dad?" Darek asked. "Tiger can't wait to be an angel, right?"

"I wanna be a shepherd."

John smiled. "You'll be a cute shepherd."

"Scary. I want to be a scary shepherd." Tiger set his fork down, put his hands on his hips, and growled.

"He's got shepherds on the brain," Ivy said.

"What are you going to be for Halloween, big guy?" Romeo asked.

"A shepherd!"

"See?" Ivy said.

Ingrid laughed.

"You know what I'm going to be?" Romeo said. "I'm going to be seventeen."

"It's your birthday?" Ivy asked.

"Yep. I'm a Halloween baby."

"I'll make you a scary cake," Ingrid said.

"So you had to choose between trick-or-treating and celebrating your birthday?" Darek said.

He shrugged. "I never really went trick-or-treating. Or celebrated my birthday. Or any holidays, really. My mom tried, but she worked a lot, and she got overtime when she worked a holiday, so . . ."

The table went quiet. Romeo took a drink. Put his glass down. "But we still celebrated. I mean, my mom would bring home leftovers from the restaurant where she worked, and one year we went to Grandma and Grandpa's house for Christmas. I'll never forget that Christmas morning. I came downstairs and Santa had been there." He looked at Tiger. "You know Santa, right?"

"I have a special stocking he puts candy in. Nana made it. It has my name on it and everything."

Romeo looked at her. "Wow. I had a stocking that Christmas too—something fuzzy and red. It didn't have my name on it. But it was a great Christmas. Just Mom and me—my brother was at his dad's. It was about a year after Eddie died, but we were okay, you know? And Mom was happy. She was . . . doing good."

He swallowed then, his voice dropping. "Yeah, that was a good Christmas."

Ingrid had stopped eating, the food in her stomach going cold, sour. She looked at John, who met her eyes with a dark expression and pursed lips.

"How about if I heat up the apple crisp, and you guys can go play some football." She cleared her plate, and the conversation behind her turned to Vikings football and their chances against the Lions.

She blinked back tears as she rinsed the plate in the sink. Why hadn't her sister replied to even one of her letters? If she'd known . . .

Romeo brought over his plate. "That was really good, Aunt Ingrid. And don't worry about a Halloween cake. But I would be happy with some of your chocolate chip cookies."

"As you wish." When she looked at him, he grinned, and she couldn't help it. She popped him a kiss, right there on his cheek.

He didn't wipe it off as he went back to the table to bus the dishes.

"Go long!" John took the ball off the line, backed up, and began to dodge Tiger as Romeo bounded through the veneer of snow toward the makeshift goal line.

John laughed, putting his hand on Tiger's head. The boy had him by the jacket.

"Grandpa, you have to fall down!"

Romeo faked one way, then sprinted the other, waving his hands. John spiraled it out to him, right in the bread-basket, and Romeo caught it a second before Darek wrapped his arms around him, slamming him to the ground.

John let Tiger take him down, grabbed the little boy, and tickled him.

"I think that was a touchdown!" Romeo said, getting up.

"I think we're going to miss kickoff," Darek said, giving him a hand. "And I think I'm too old for this."

"*You're* too old?" John said. "Whatever. Tiger, push Grandpa off the ground."

Tiger put all his weight into John's shoulder, grunting. "You're too big!"

John hauled him over his shoulder like a sack of grain as Tiger laughed. "Look, another football!"

Darek came running up, and John flipped Tiger into

his arms. "A handoff!" He let Darek carry the rascal into the house. They'd made a mess of the snow, but he could admit that Ingrid's suggestion had loosened the tension in him from lunch.

Romeo had the power to steal his wife's heart right out from under her, and frankly John could feel himself losing the battle to hold back his own affection for the kid. But Romeo had a future that they had no right to, and John needed to keep that in the forefront of his brain. In the meantime, maybe he could step up and help give the boy what he needed—freedom and the opportunity to make something of himself.

Away from the vices and mistakes of his mother.

Romeo walked over, a flush to his cheeks. "Great game. You might have played defensive end, but you throw like a quarterback."

"And you have soft hands, kid. You could be a wideout if you wanted."

Romeo flipped John the ball.

John caught it, lined up his fingers along the laces. "In fact, you could do anything you wanted. Including join the military. I've been thinking about it, and I'd be happy to sign the papers for your emancipation, if you'd like. Ingrid says you're doing well in school. You could get your GED and enlist, maybe even be stationed near your brother."

Romeo had stopped, his expression enigmatic. "Oh."

John frowned. "Isn't that what you want? You said you did—or at least I thought the social worker mentioned it—"

"Yeah. Sure. Whatever. That's awesome, man. Thanks." He extended a hand to John, but the handshake felt weak, fast. "I'll talk to the school, see when the next GED test is."

He took off for the house, leaving John in the muddied snow.

Inside, the house smelled like gingerbread, thanks to the candle Ingrid had lit on the kitchen counter. He toed off his boots, drawn by the sounds of football and laughter in the den. Darek had pulled Tiger onto his lap, and Ivy was curled up beside them as they listened to the pregame show.

Romeo sat on the floor, petting Butter, the dog's head on his lap. He tousled her ear as if it were an old habit.

"Where's your aunt?"

Romeo shrugged.

"I think she's upstairs? Or maybe in the basement? I dunno," Ivy said. She laid her head on Darek's shoulder, closed her eyes.

John glanced at the time—five minutes to kickoff—and headed upstairs.

She wasn't in their bedroom, so he descended the stairs to the finished basement. Or partially finished. They'd thrown down a remnant carpet, painted the cinderblock walls, and stored their old furniture. The kids had used it for years as a gaming/television room, and it smelled moist and clammy.

He noticed a light streaming from the storage area near the furnace room. "Ingrid?"

Nothing. He walked closer and poked his head in.

She sat on a box, another open at her feet, a pile of red-and-white felt in her hands.

"What's going on?"

She took a breath that sounded tremulous. And when she looked up, forcing a smile, he'd have to be an idiot not to notice she'd been crying.

"Honey?" He came in, knelt in front of her.

She wiped the moisture from her face. "It's nothing. Silly, really. I'm fine."

He touched her hand. "You don't look fine."

"I just miss the kids." She stood. "I think I'll box up a few of Grace's and Eden's ornaments and send them down to the girls so they have some for their Christmas celebrations. And Darek will need his for his tree."

"I'm sure they'd like that. . . ."

Reaching into the box, she pulled out an open craft kit stuffed with thread and felt and sequins. She inserted the felt into the kit, then held on to it as she closed the box and shoved it back under the shelf.

"What's that?" He gestured to the kit.

"Just an old stocking kit. I thought I'd finish making it for Romeo."

"Ingrid—"

She held up her hand. "For him to take with him, John. I know he'll be leaving, but you heard him—the boy never had a stocking of his own. Everyone needs to have their own stocking. It's a reminder that they're loved." She pushed past him. "Isn't the game starting soon?"

"Yeah . . ." But he didn't follow her. Instead, he leaned down and looked at the box, examining the scribbling on the outside that labeled it.

He heard his wife's step on the stairs as she went to join the family. But he couldn't move. Couldn't think.

He had no words, just the swish of his heart in his ears.

For Benjamin.

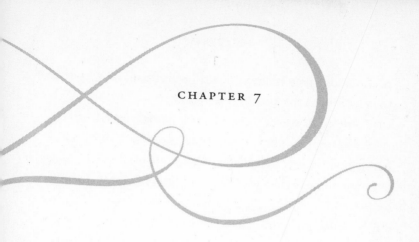

CHAPTER 7

INGRID COULDN'T EXACTLY put her finger on it, but somehow, over the past week, a switch had flipped in Romeo.

He'd gone from being the charmer to the boy she'd expected—aloof, angry . . . trouble. He no longer greeted her when he came home and had even shut Butter out of his room. Ingrid had found the dog sleeping in the hallway outside his door the last two nights.

Lifting a shoulder to hold the phone against her ear, she opened the oven and pulled out a tray of chocolate chip cookies. A birthday treat that she hoped might shake him out of his funk. Outside, the weather had turned pale and bleak, the temperatures dropping. Trick-or-treaters would show up in parkas—if they made the trek to the resort at all. Usually she left the lights off and went to town to celebrate at the community party.

Tonight, however, they'd have a party here.

A full-out jamboree, if she could end this call with a holy family lined up for the live Nativity. Jason and Nicole Backlund would be perfect for Mary and Joseph, and their eight-month-old would make an adorable baby Jesus. "I know it'll be cold, but you can wear warm clothes under your costumes, and little Neil will be all toasty in his snowsuit—"

"I don't think so, Mrs. Christiansen. Jason's family has their annual Christmas Eve party, and we haven't attended the live Nativity in years."

Right. "Okay, thank you." She hung up and crossed the Backlunds off her very short list.

She set the cookies to cool and headed to the entry, grabbing her jacket, her UGGs. The phone rang just as she retrieved her keys. She picked it up in case it was John.

"Ingrid, hey, it's Seb. I wanted to talk to John about Romeo."

"John's in town, and I'm just headed out to pick up Romeo from practice."

"That's the thing. . . . Uh, Romeo wasn't at practice today."

She sat down on the bench. "What?"

"I didn't want to mention this, but he wasn't at practice yesterday either. And he showed up late two days before that. I haven't talked to Coach Knight, but my guess is that he's probably off the team."

"No, Seb—he's worked so hard."

"For a month, yeah. And frankly we could use him in the game tomorrow. But you can't ditch the team and expect to show up and play."

"Of course not. I'm just—"

"Ingrid, is everything okay with him? Because at practice on Monday, I barely recognized him. He played angry, then picked a fight with another player, and I heard a string of words out of his mouth I had never heard him use. Is he okay?"

"Maybe he misses his mom. I'll find him. Thanks, Seb."

She hung up and closed the door behind her. What could Romeo be thinking? And if John discovered he'd missed practice . . .

Just in case he'd returned to the school, she went there first. The school was dark, so she drove down to Licks and Stuff, searched for him through the windows, then headed over to the Java Cup. How many places could a kid hang out after school in a town this size?

Maybe he'd gone to the community Halloween party?

She parked outside the community center, walked in, and stood for a moment, swept back to the days when her children dressed as hoboes and Jedi and pirates. She jumped out of the way of two zombies and moved toward the cookie table.

No Romeo.

Ingrid walked back outside, a rock in her stomach. *Please, Lord.* She didn't know when it had happened, but he felt like her own son, the worry for him as tangible as it might have been for Casper or Owen.

When her cell phone rang, she dug it out of her pocket.

"Hey, it's me. I'm still in town. I thought I'd swing by the school and pick up Romeo."

John. She took a breath. "Actually, I'm in town too. Um . . ."

"What's the matter, Ingrid?"

Oh, why was it that when it came to the kids, he could read her mind? "Nothing—"

"Tell me." His tone turned solemn, and for a moment, they were once again, standing by Darek when he told them the news of his pregnant girlfriend, gathering at Owen's side in the hospital when his career might be over, or even watching their two youngest sons brawl on Eden's wedding day.

"He's missing, John."

Silence. Then, "Define *missing*."

"He didn't show up for practice today." Or yesterday, but she didn't want to add that.

"How many days has he missed?"

She sighed. "Two. But he's been upset for a few days."

"I'll find him."

"John—"

"Ingrid, listen, I could have told you this kid was trouble."

"That's not fair. He was doing great and then something—"

"He's a time bomb waiting to go off. I'm surprised it took this long. You can't blame him for being an emotional wreck just like his mother."

"Well, maybe she wouldn't be if someone actually cared. If someone stopped to listen instead of shutting the door in her face." She didn't mean to shout, wasn't sure where the anger came from, but listening to Romeo's stories and knowing they could have done something had seeded a growing ache inside her.

But maybe this fight wasn't entirely about Romeo. Or his mother.

And that realization turned her silent, the wounds searing.

John's voice was quiet. "I was trying to protect us. I did what I thought was best."

Maybe he wasn't talking about Kari either.

"I'm sure you did," Ingrid said softly. "But the best thing for Romeo is for us to find him and care enough to listen." She watched the waves turn the shore frothy.

"Let me just find him first. Where are you?"

"I'm in the—"

He drove up beside her in his truck, cell phone to his ear. She hung up.

He let his truck run, and they stared at each other through the windows.

Her phone rang again and she looked at the screen, frowning at the number for the vet clinic. "Kate?"

"Hey, Ingrid. Uh . . . I have a situation here, and I was hoping you could come down—"

"What's going on?"

John had gotten out of the truck.

"I caught Romeo breaking into my office today, and the police are here—"

"We'll be right there."

Ingrid grimaced as she relayed the information to John, then followed him in her Caravan the two blocks to the vet's office.

A cruiser, with lights flashing, was parked outside.

Oh, Romeo.

She got out and followed John in. Romeo sat, hand-cuffed, on a bench by the door. Shoulders slumped, head down, hands in his pockets, wearing just a thin sweatshirt. Ingrid made a note to dig up a warmer jacket for him. Kyle Hueston, their local deputy, was taking a statement from Kate, who gave Ingrid a pained glance.

"What happened?" John said, and to her eyes, Romeo paled at the sight of him. His expression made Ingrid want to cry. He looked thirteen, lost, even afraid.

"I'm not sure. Nothing is broken, but I heard the dogs barking in the back, and when I turned on the light, I found Romeo in the outside kennels," Kate said.

"You broke into an animal shelter?" John said, his voice rising. Ingrid gripped his arm.

Romeo looked away, his jaw tight. "I just wanted to see the dogs."

"Listen, I don't want to press charges," Kate said. "But—"

"I have an idea," Kyle said. "Maybe we could work something out. A work exchange?"

"Yeah, what if Romeo helped clean the kennels? Maybe assisted me with some of the dogs after school?"

"He has football," John said, and Ingrid said nothing. "But he could donate his Saturdays."

He turned to Romeo, who wore such a drained, almost-incredulous look that Ingrid wanted to put her arms around him. In a blink, his face closed up. He lifted a shoulder in a shrug.

"Okay, then. Saturday, 9 a.m.?" John said.

Romeo nodded, and Kyle uncuffed him.

"Thanks, Kate," Ingrid said as she followed John and Romeo outside.

But John stopped him by the truck. "Romeo, you have some explaining to do. What's going on?"

"Leave me alone. I want to see my mom."

His words landed like a blow.

"You know she can't see you right now," Ingrid said.

"I don't care. I . . . I don't want to be here anymore."

The words hollowed Ingrid out. She shoved her hands into her pockets, fighting the bite of the wind.

"You missed practice." John stepped in front of him. "Listen, you don't just start something, then quit. Your team needs you."

Ingrid reached out, wanting to press her hand to John's arm. Because in Romeo's world, people *did* start things, only to quit.

And that's when truth appeared in Romeo's eyes. His voice turned sharp and raw. "I know you don't want me around really, so what do you care if I play football or not?"

Ingrid wrapped her arms around her waist. "What are you talking about?"

But Romeo turned away. "It doesn't matter."

"I do care if you play football," John said quietly. "And we do want you around, Romeo. You're our responsibility."

Romeo didn't look at him. "Not for long. I checked into the GED. I'm taking the test if you're still signing the papers."

Ingrid stilled. "What is he talking about, John?"

John ignored her. "That's your decision, son. But until then, you have a couple of games left and a team you made promises to." He put his hand on Romeo's shoulder. "Let's go talk to the coach and see if he'll let you back on the team."

Ingrid stared hard at John as he turned Romeo toward the truck. She wanted to make him stop, tell her what he'd done.

"I'll see you at home, Ingrid," he said.

"John!"

But they got into his truck, and Romeo shut the door, not looking at her as John drove out of the parking lot.

She stood there, watching him pull away, shivering as the cold twined through her body, the wind turning her brittle. She stiffened, forced a smile.

Even though, in the air, she could smell a winter storm brewing on the far-off horizon.

John had found himself again by the time he finished loading the dishwasher, scraping the remains of beef brisket into the sink, washing the Crock-Pot, and sweeping the floor.

The simple tasks helped him untie the knot in his chest, or at least breathe freely.

Whatever reason Ingrid had for keeping Romeo's behavior a secret, he wanted to hear it. He'd be patient. And then he'd fix the jagged rift between them that seemed to have ripped open this afternoon.

If he hadn't recognized signs of trouble when he left Ingrid at Kate's office and marched Romeo over to Coach Knight's house to apologize, he recognized it when he arrived home to find the table set, food on the stove, and a note on the counter indicating that she'd already eaten.

She left out a birthday card and a plate of cookies for

Romeo, who had stared at them as if he'd just taken a hit to the gut.

John served Romeo and himself, and they ate in strained silence. He hoped Romeo spent supper pondering his second chance.

Although he would have to sit out Friday's game, he'd be allowed back for the play-offs if they won.

But Romeo had destroyed the fragile trust between them, and John informed the sullen kid that after football ended, he'd spend every afternoon helping to build Darek's house. And Saturdays at the animal shelter, cleaning up after the dogs.

In fact, John intended to keep the kid in his sights until the moment his brother knocked on the door. He wouldn't put it past Romeo to go AWOL, hitchhike his way to Duluth, and get murdered on the side of the road. Not on his watch, thank you.

Romeo had headed upstairs with his backpack full of homework immediately after supper. John noticed Butter following him, heard the door close upstairs.

Once he'd cleaned up and emptied the dustpan, he slipped on his boots and took the trash outside. The wind carried the sting of sleet, and it bit into his skin as he opened the gate to the trash area, dropped the bag into the Dumpster. Overhead, a pitch-black sky blotted out the stars, and in the distance, a lonely wolf—or perhaps one of the sled dogs from nearby camps—howled in mourning.

He hustled back inside, thankful for his warm, dry home, and slipped off his boots. Flicking off the lights in the kitchen, he headed upstairs.

Light streamed out from under the door to his room. He took a long breath, then eased the door open.

Ingrid sat on the floor, her craft supplies scattered around her, a tall light pulled close to illuminate her stocking project. A dozen white, brown, and red shapes—cut out and organized into piles—surrounded her, along with tiny containers of sequins, colored thread strung around cardboard, and various pieces of stocking already constructed. She had her earbuds in, swaying to what he supposed was music as she worked a needle and thread.

She wore black yoga pants and a red T-shirt over a long-sleeved white shirt. He recognized the tee as one of Amelia's, the one with Rudolph on the front. A stocking cap—red and fuzzy—held her hair back, letting it curl out the bottom.

So Ingrid. No one did Christmas like his wife, and in an instant, the final vestiges of his frustration vanished.

He shut the door, and she looked up, popped one of her earbuds out. "Is he in his room?"

"Yeah." John sat on the edge of the bed. Took a breath. "I think we're in for a storm tonight."

She looked back at her work but nodded.

"Do you think you'll finish by the time his brother arrives?"

She lifted a shoulder, then reached out and handed him the kit cover. "I know it's a little young for him—Santa on a sled, holding a bear—but it's very northern Minnesota, and . . . well, it's what I had."

He stared at the picture. "I know . . . I know it was Benjamin's."

"Yes. But Benjamin doesn't need it, does he?" She swallowed, looked away. "He's with Jesus."

John frowned, nonplussed at her words. "We need to talk about what happened today, Ingrid. You should have told me Romeo skipped practice."

She pulled the other earbud out. "I just found out today. But maybe you want to tell me what he meant about getting his GED?"

She kept her tone light, but he could spot an ambush. Although he wasn't quite sure what he'd done wrong. "I offered to agree to his emancipation. I figured it's the least I could do for him. Help him have his future."

She put the earbud back in. Nodded.

"Ingrid, I'm not sure what's going on here—"

"I got an e-mail from Casper today. He's staying in Roatán for Christmas. I admit I was holding out hope that he might come home. . . . Can you imagine? The Caribbean for Christmas."

Uh, yeah. In fact he'd imagined a lot for them. And frankly he couldn't figure out why those dreams felt so far away.

He slid off the bed and moved to sit facing her. She didn't look at him.

"Honey, are you angry with me?"

She gave him a tight smile that didn't meet her eyes. "Why would you think that?"

Why would he—? "Because I'm not an idiot. Because it feels like no matter what I do, it makes you angry. Because even though I've let Romeo into our home, you still act like I don't want him here."

"Do you?"

"I just don't want you to get hurt. The more you grow attached to this kid, the more it's going to hurt when he leaves."

"Motherhood is about letting go, John. I'm not ignorant of the fact that my children are leaving me. In fact, I want them to. I've spent my entire life preparing them to leave me. I'm ready to get hurt. What I don't want is to spend every moment that Romeo is here guarding my heart. I want to savor him being here." She put down her sewing. "We can't live our lives trying to protect ourselves from getting hurt. And you can't live your life trying to protect me."

But . . . wasn't that his job?

He reached out, touched her face, let his fingers run down her cheekbone. He expected her to lean into his touch, to meet his eyes, perhaps offer an invitation.

Instead, she focused on her sewing. He watched her fingers make one tiny stitch after another.

He dropped his hand. "I'm supposed to protect you, Ingrid. That's my job."

A tear dripped off her chin onto the felt. She swallowed, pressed her thumb into the moisture.

He stared at it in horror. "Tell me what I did, and I'll fix it. Please."

Only then did she look up at him, her eyes red. She shook her head. "I don't think you can ever fix it, John."

Then she put down the stocking, got up, and headed to the door.

He stared after her, his breath hot in his chest. What—?
He couldn't help but follow her.

She went to Romeo's room and cracked open the door.
The light streamed in over Romeo, curled up under the
sheets of Owen's bed. Butter lay at the foot of the bed, and
she lifted her head as if to say, *I got this. All is well.*

Ingrid closed the door. "I was hoping you could fix
Romeo. But now I'm not so sure you can, even if you
wanted to."

Then she walked away and left him standing in the hallway, her words like fists in his chest. *Even if you wanted to.*

CHAPTER 8

No one told John that he couldn't fix something. Not his marriage. Not Romeo. And certainly not the decrepit box for the Nativity scene the community called a stable.

"Hold the door open. I just need to grab this wood, and we'll be out of here."

Romeo held open the door to the shed behind the community center as John pulled out another section of the manger scene he'd finally tracked down.

Nate had only mentioned that the stable might need some work, but what did John expect from a Realtor?

"What is this thing?"

"It's a barn. Sort of." John would have to rebuild the entire stage. The structure fell apart as soon as he and Romeo pulled it from the shed. The roof hung in pieces and the ends of the display sagged, unable to hold up anything.

He set the boards on the ground, stood back to survey the damage. "It's where we host the Nativity scene. But it's not looking too good, is it?"

Romeo gave it a kick. He wore one of the boys' old work jackets and an orange stocking cap. In the week since football ended, he'd helped John every day after school, as decreed, and they'd managed to get Darek's house under roof, tarping it off for shingles in the spring. In the meantime, Darek would work inside.

John had taught Romeo how to run a table saw, a Skilsaw, and a nail gun, how to measure twice and cut once, and the basics of framing a house.

The kid listened as if he were preparing to appear on *Surviorman*, asked to live in the wild.

Ingrid's words settled into John's brain like glue. *I was hoping you could fix Romeo. But now I'm not so sure you can, even if you wanted to.*

If he wanted to. He couldn't deny the fact that he enjoyed Romeo's company. And the boy worked hard, without complaint, at home and at the animal shelter, according to Kate.

Slowly, over the past three weeks, John had seen the

kid emerge from his shell. John even got him behind the wheel for the first time in his life and took him driving on the back roads.

Yeah, he could admit he hoped this mystery brother didn't show up anytime soon. Ingrid had managed to contact the social worker regarding a visit to Romeo's mother, but she reminded them there could be no visits until after Thanksgiving. And by her tone, apparently even that might be too soon.

E-mails to Matthew remained unanswered.

Ingrid's hopes just might materialize—Romeo in their home for Christmas.

John secretly began to hope for it too. In a couple weeks the ice would be thick enough to skate on, and maybe he'd even take the kid snowmobiling.

As for his wife . . . *I don't think you can ever fix it, John.*

Fix what? Their fractured family? A lonely Christmas? Perhaps, but he could try. The live Nativity display he drew up would be legendary, and if that didn't prove to his wife that he could buy into her need to stick around, celebrate Christmas even without their family, he didn't know what would.

He glanced at Romeo. "Grab that end. We'll get it up to the resort and see what we can salvage."

Romeo leaned down, grabbed the edge, lifted. They dragged it over and tossed it into the back of the truck, went back for the rest of the pieces. As John closed the tailgate, Romeo climbed into the cab, blowing on his hands. "I can't wait for that turkey."

Him, either. Ingrid had been in the kitchen basting the Thanksgiving bird when they left. Ivy and Darek wouldn't be heading over until this evening, but still, he had to wonder how he'd landed right here, dragging around a busted barn in the middle of a football Thursday. He had an idea who might be the real turkey.

But he refused to let his marriage—or Romeo—go down on his watch.

"You suppose the Lions are winning?"

John glanced at Romeo. "Let's not think about it."

A hearty two inches of snow blanketed the ground. Winter had gusted in last week with slate-gray skies, an ice storm, and below-zero temperatures on the eve of the second play-off game of the season.

The Huskies lost by one touchdown, and even John couldn't hate the fact that the cold hours in the stands had ended.

He pulled out, headed home. If he worked hard, he could get the frame rebuilt by tonight and have the structure constructed in parts by Sunday. Then he'd have to shingle it—he had some shakes left over from the cabins. Finally he'd paint it, string lights, and—his brain child—install heaters along the base. He'd heard Ingrid on the phone and knew the prospect of standing in the cold for an hour scared off any potential Nativity family.

But if he could offer them warmth . . . he might not just save his own marriage with his stable, but someone else's as well.

"Why a barn?" Romeo asked.

"Well, I guess it's more of a stable, and in real life, it was supposedly a cave, but we work with what we have."

Silence.

He looked at Romeo. "What?"

"Tell me again why we're building a barn?"

"Because that's where Mary gave birth? She put the baby in a manger?"

"Oh." Romeo looked away, tucked his hands under his arms.

"You do know the story, right?"

Romeo offered one of his signature shrugs.

Seriously? "Romeo, did anyone tell you the real story of Christmas?"

"I thought it was about Santa."

John cut down Main Street. Already holly and pine boughs decorated the lamps along the street, a holiday glow upon the crystalline snow. This weekend, a glittering tree would appear in the park off the harbor.

"Santa is an add-on. The real story is about God sending His Son to earth to save us from ourselves. We celebrate His birth at Christmas."

"Oh, right. Mary and Joseph and some angels. I thought it was a fairy tale."

The story, the gospel, embedded John's bones, as familiar as breathing. He tried not to take offense at Romeo's almost-mocking tone. "It's not a fairy tale, and that's what this live Nativity is all about—to make it real. To put ourselves in Mary and Joseph's place and get a new perspective. Imagine you're about to get married and the girl you love tells you she's going to have a baby."

"I'd be pretty mad."

"Yeah, and then she tells you the baby is God's. And He's going to save the world. Crazy, right?"

Romeo regarded him with a frown.

"Exactly. So you don't believe her, until an angel appears and tells you that not only is Mary telling the truth, but you're supposed to marry her and be the father to this baby."

"So Joseph wasn't the real father?" Romeo held his hands in front of the heater.

"He was Jesus' earthly father."

"But I'll bet he didn't want to be. Raising someone else's kid? No guy wants that." Romeo said it without rancor, just matter-of-fact. "At least that's what my mom said after Eddie left."

Huh. John turned onto the highway. "I thought you said he died."

A muscle pulled in his jaw as Romeo shook his head. "It's just easier that way. To think he got sick and died. And he took the dog too."

John suddenly wanted to clamp the kid's shoulder, maybe even wrap an arm around him. Especially when Ingrid's voice haunted him. *But now I'm not so sure you can, even if you wanted to.*

Oh, he wanted to. But he was in way over his head.

"I think Joseph took it pretty seriously. He took Mary as his wife and protected Jesus like a father would. Saved His life a couple of times, just because he listened to God."

But it had to be overwhelming, when John thought about it. As he held his own son in his arms at the Deep Haven hospital, his knees had nearly buckled at the responsibility. And every child after that had shaken him to his core.

So much on his shoulders, sometimes it felt like it could crumple him.

Imagine raising the Son of God.

"So why Joseph?" Romeo asked.

"What?" John turned onto a dirt road. Snow blanketed the bushy pine trees, a trail of white that, under a starry sky, might feel magical.

"Why did God pick Joseph to raise His kid? I mean, what did Joseph have that made him so special?"

"I don't know. I've never thought about it."

John pulled into the driveway. Christmas lights bordered the doorway, the edge of the roof, twinkling in the twilight, beckoning them home. Darek's doing—a hint of cheer for the resort pictures he'd taken to post online.

"Let's get the barn unloaded; then we'll check on the game." He got out. Romeo's door shut on the other side.

Romeo began to unload boards. "We slept in our car once. My mom cried all night long."

John glanced at him, but Romeo didn't seem embarrassed, just continued working.

"Imagine how awful Joseph had to feel for his wife to give birth in a barn. Yuck."

John picked up some boards, shouldered them, and brought them to his freshly built garage.

Romeo's words needled him. Yeah. It would be humbling, especially for a young man hoping to provide for his family.

"Let's put the boards back here." He opened the garage doors and pointed to the workshop in back. Romeo carried his armful in and dropped them on the floor.

John dropped his own boards as Romeo moved past him on his way for another load. John stopped him with a hand on his shoulder, his chest suddenly thick, cottony. He met Romeo's eyes, level with his own.

"You won't ever sleep in a car again, Romeo. You're a part of this family, whether you like it or not, and you'll always have a place here."

Romeo blinked, swallowed. Looked away.

John clamped him around the back of his neck, drew his head to his shoulder. Slapped him on the back fast, then let him go. "Get us another load."

Romeo nodded and stepped away quickly.

John flicked on the light and began to stack the boards. He had a few decent two-by-fours, a two-by-six he could saw in half. The rest he'd use to construct a new manger. Yeah, he could fix this.

He glanced outside. "Romeo?"

What was taking the kid so long? He saw the truck's headlights, although he thought he'd turned them off. And saw Romeo outlined against them. He simply stood there.

Then another figure stepped into the lights.

John headed outside when the two figures embraced.

"Hello?" His chest had already tightened, his stomach burning as he moved into the light.

Romeo stepped back from the man, and John recognized a military bearing despite the beard, the black baseball hat. He had Romeo's eyes and high cheekbones and wore an Army-green jacket, jeans, black boots.

As if he'd just stepped off the transport from Afghanistan.

The man extended his hand. "Hi, Uncle John. I don't know if you remember me. I'm Matthew—Romeo's big brother."

This just might be the worst Thanksgiving Ingrid had ever endured. And that counted the year Darek, Casper, and Grace all had the flu and lost their dinners on the family room carpet. Or even the year of the great storm that shut off the power halfway through the roasting of the turkey.

She'd made a festive meal of pumpkin pie, chocolate milk, and Jell-O salad.

No, nothing compared to the misery of watching Romeo's half brother woo him with stories of the military. The camaraderie, the adventure.

The danger.

She fabricated a smile and managed to ask appropriate questions, to nod without censure, and even to not chuck an entire pie into Matthew's too-handsome face.

"We tried to get ahold of you, Matthew," she mentioned later that night as they played their annual family game of Sorry! and she mercilessly sent him back to start.

"I'm sorry. It's hard to get e-mail sometimes. But I got them and, of course, stopped by to see Mom on my way here."

"They let you see her?" Romeo asked, sending a frown toward Ingrid. Like she made up the rules?

"They weren't going to, but they made an exception because I'm just back from deployment." He drew a one and put his piece back out on the board. Of course.

"How is she?"

"Missing you, pal. But okay. I think she's going to be in there for a while, though. She's lost a lot of weight, and they have her on antidepressants."

Ingrid glanced at John, begging him to stay silent. But he seemed to have his own thoughts, based on the way he eyed Matthew. Especially when Matthew suggested he and Romeo hit the road for a couple of weeks and head down to Disney World.

Yeah, she wanted to strangle hero-boy, then, for the way Romeo brightened up.

"You'd think Santa Claus arrived right on our doorstep, a month early," she said to John later as she put lotion on her arms. He burrowed under the covers, his eyes closed. A chill had settled over the house, frost already scrolling up the windows. She climbed under the covers, tucking them in around her. "I mean, I expected him, but . . . he can't be serious. Romeo has school, and he can't just take off with Matthew. Disney World costs a fortune. How come Matthew has that kind of money?"

"We can't trap the kid here, Ingrid—"

"What are you talking about? We're his legal guardians. He can't go anywhere without our permission."

He opened one eye then. "You do realize he wants to join the military, right? Be an emancipated minor—"

She held up a hand. "Don't get me started on that hare-brained idea. Seriously, would you let one of your boys drop out of school to go to Disney World?"

"If he was going to take his GED—"

"And join the military? At seventeen?"

He sighed. "Listen, honey, I don't like it any more than you do, but he has to make his own choices."

"Just tell me, John: would you let your son do it?"

"He's not my son."

"But see, right now he is. He's legally your son, and clearly you've forgotten that."

John opened both eyes now. "Ingrid. I like the boy—I really do. And frankly I was hoping he would stay for Christmas. But he's *not* my son. He's not *our* son. He's just a boy who—"

"Who God gave us to love and care for."

He stared at her, a slow frown creasing his face.

"I know you weren't in the market for another gig as father, but like it or not, you've been given a rare opportunity to care about Romeo, and I think he cares about you too." She blinked hard, fighting the rise of emotion.

He sat up, put his hand on her back. "I know you wanted him here—that in a way, he filled a void, but—"

She shook her head. Drew in a breath. "Do you know what today is, John?"

"Thanksgiving?"

She looked away, catching her lip in her bottom teeth. "It's Benjamin's due date."

He said nothing. Then, "Ingrid . . ."

"It's okay. I know you don't really think about it. But I do. Every year. And this year . . . this year it felt as if Romeo was sort of . . . well, the son we should have had."

Silly. Stupid. Even desperate. She pressed her cheeks, feeling the moisture there. "Just don't let him leave. I don't trust Matthew—something's not right. Please."

"I don't know what I can do, Ingrid."

She closed her eyes. "Yes, you do. Fix it, John. Please, just fix this."

Fix it, John.

The words hung in his head as he finished adding the last of the shakes to the half roof of the stable. He didn't know exactly what, however, he had to fix.

Matthew hadn't mentioned Disney World once in the last three days and, in fact, hung around like he might be staying forever. He'd helped John and Romeo build the stable and had strung the lights around the outside of the frame.

Sure, the man reminded him of Kari, back in the day

when she could charm her way into people's trust, then break their hearts. Carefree, even reckless. The fact that Kari had settled down with Matthew's father, at least for a while, seemed a miracle.

"How many tours have you completed, Matthew?" John picked up the thermos of hot cocoa.

"This was my fourth," he said. "But maybe not my last."

Romeo looked at him. "Really?"

Matthew lifted a shoulder, a familiar Young family gesture. He handed John his cup. "You headed inside? I'd love more of those cookies if there are any left."

But John didn't move. "Matthew. Help me understand something. Are you . . . are you staying stateside, or are you just on leave?"

Matthew grabbed a hammer, tossed it in his grip. "On leave."

Romeo stood. "You're going back?"

"In two weeks, yeah. I thought I told you that. Two weeks, we zip down to Disney World; then I'm back in the sand."

"And Romeo?"

Matthew looked at John. "Uh, Romeo's a big boy. He can take care of himself."

Ingrid's words had niggled at him for the past three

days, and now he knew why. *I don't trust Matthew—something's not right.*

After thirty years, a man should trust his wife's sixth sense. "Matthew, I'm afraid your trip isn't going to work for Romeo. Or us."

Romeo rounded on him. "What?"

"Romeo, you can't drop out of school to hang out with your brother—especially since he's leaving in two weeks. Then what?"

"You said I'd always . . ." Romeo bit his lip.

John's words flooded back to him. *Have a place here.*

John drew in a long breath. "As your legal guardian, I need to tell you that leaving is not okay. You can't just take off—"

"Because if I do, I can't come back, right?"

"I didn't say that."

"You don't have to. Listen, dude. I don't need a father—I've done fine for seventeen years without one, so you can just—"

He spit out a word that should have made John wince. But he just stared at the teen, sadness sweeping through him.

It was Owen all over again. Angry, frustrated. Needing someone to step in. But Owen was twenty-one.

Romeo needed more from John than what he'd given Owen.

"You're not going."

"Oh yes, I am." He dropped his hammer and stormed out of the shed.

Matthew had whisked off his hat, held it between clenched hands. "I didn't . . . I mean . . ."

"He needs someone who is going to stick around in his life right now."

Matthew nodded. "I get that."

"And that's not you, is it?"

Matthew shook his head. Sighed. "I think I'm going to get my stuff."

"Matt—"

"No, I gotta get going anyway. The Disney thing . . . Probably that was just a dream anyway. I got buddies waiting for me in Minneapolis."

John stilled. "Wait. You weren't even planning on taking him to Disney World?"

Matthew made a face. "It just sort of came out, and then I was stuck in the lie, and it kept getting bigger and bigger and . . . But I was thinking about it."

"What, were you going to sneak out in the middle of the night, not tell him—? Oh, my. You were."

Matthew's jaw tightened.

"I'm not sure what they're teaching you in the military, son, but that's not what honor is."

"Whatever. Tell Romeo I said bye." He brushed past John.

"Matthew, don't you dare leave Romeo without saying good-bye yourself."

But Matthew ignored him and headed to the house. John wanted to throw one of the mugs after him. Or worse.

Instead, he followed him inside, set the mugs and the thermos on the counter.

Ingrid looked up from where she sat, phone in her hand, the church directory open on the counter. "What happened?"

"I fixed it," he said quietly.

Her eyes widened when she saw Matthew appear moments later, his duffel slung over his shoulder.

"Romeo," she said, glancing at John.

Matthew said nothing as he stormed out of the house.

"Romeo!" she shouted, getting off the stool.

But by the time Romeo made it back downstairs, Matthew had pulled out. Romeo didn't bother with shoes, just banged through the door, running out into the snow and ice in his stocking feet.

"Matthew!"

The night closed around Matthew's red taillights.

John stood there a moment, watching as Romeo stared into the darkness. Ingrid touched his back, but he shook her away.

John went to the door. "Romeo, come inside."

Romeo marched past him. At the foot of the stairs, he turned, glaring first at Ingrid, then at John. "You're not my parents."

Then he headed upstairs. Ingrid pressed a hand to her mouth.

"Yeah, I really fixed it," John said.

CHAPTER 9

INGRID DIDN'T KNOW WHY she tried so hard when everything she did seemed to backfire. She pressed End on her cell phone and set it on the counter in the fellowship hall kitchen.

She'd single-handedly managed to drive the last nail in the coffin of the live Nativity.

"It's over. The Westerlinds have sold all their goats and are moving to Florida. And there isn't a bunny to be found in the county, let alone a sheep. And I've tapped out all the young couples on the Mary and Joseph list." She set her head in the cradle of her arms.

"Aw, c'mon. You can't find anyone to stand outside in below-freezing temperatures? Shocker." Ellie walked by, carrying a handful of hangers with angel wings attached.

Edith and her hospitality crew had decked out the church for tomorrow's live Nativity.

"Maybe we should stick a doll in the manger, dress up a couple of mannequins, and make it all about the angels," Ingrid said, offering a lopsided smile to Annalise, who had engineered the cookie drive and now assembled trays for the exchange.

Annalise swiped a gingerbread cookie from the tray, handing it to Ingrid. "Have some sugar. I think you're starting to get delirious."

Ingrid took the cookie. "I just want to leave town. Maybe I should have taken John up on his offer to go to Europe. It's not sounding so crazy now."

"How is Amelia?"

"Fabulous. Going skiing in Switzerland with friends over the holidays. I'm sure we would have cramped her style, tromping around Prague. But Paris would have been fun."

Maybe. The idea of standing in the frigid wind above Paris as they renewed their vows seemed more ironic than romantic, however. Their entire marriage had turned frosty over the past three weeks, thanks to her belief that she could somehow mother Romeo into wholeness. She should have learned her lesson—she couldn't even mother her own family into healing. She'd never seen her brood so fractured—Casper in Roatán, living the life of a pirate on the Caribbean. Eden and Grace in Minneapolis, starting their own lives. Amelia storming Europe, and Owen . . . who knew where?

Her last letter had come back *Return to sender, address unknown.* And he hadn't responded to any of her Facebook messages. Only his recent phone call to Eden, and the confirmation that he had headed west to Vancouver to stay with some hockey pals, kept Ingrid from losing her mind.

Please, Lord, let him be okay.

"It would be a shame to cancel the live Nativity after John built that fortress." Annalise added a cup of tea to Ingrid's cookie therapy. "I think Mary might have preferred it over the stable Joseph found for her. Did I see baseboard patio heaters attached to the stable?"

"Yeah. We used them for the deck, back when the resort hosted a Christmas open house. They actually keep the area pretty warm."

"And lights? And a new manger?"

Ingrid nodded. John had thrown himself into the transformation of the rickety community prop, rebuilding it into work of art. She had to give him kudos for that. Even if he couldn't fix their marriage, he could build her one mean stable.

A regular Joseph.

He'd even added a painted sign advertising the event for everyone driving by. An event that would be missing a holy family.

As Annalise returned to organizing the cookies, Noelle brought her own cup of tea over. She wore a pair of jeans with a gaudy Christmas sweater. Ingrid eyed it, made a face. Noelle made a face back at her. "I found it in the back of the closet and decided to embrace the ugly-sweater trend."

"Hmm. Maybe don't embrace it quite so heartily," Ingrid said.

Noelle laughed. "How's Romeo? I didn't see him in church last week."

"He's angry. Sullen. Not talking to us. He hasn't forgiven us for driving his brother away, as he puts in. And his mother isn't helping—she's struggling through her treatment. Romeo called the social worker a week ago and asked to be moved. She said that she'd try to find him a new placement, but I think it's probably not easy so close to Christmas."

She tried to deliver her report without her throat closing up, but she looked away, blinked hard. "I feel terrible. It's hard enough hearing about my sister's horrible life and the choices she's made that have so wounded Romeo, but knowing I could have helped her . . ."

"What are you talking about?"

"She wanted to live with us after Romeo was born. But John said no. We'd just . . . lost a baby. And he thought it would be too hard. I didn't even know she'd called until weeks later when my parents mentioned it. By that time, she wasn't talking to me." Ingrid picked up her phone, began to scroll through names. "I wrote to her numerous times, but she wouldn't answer."

"That's on her, not you."

"I know . . . but I thought taking Romeo in would be a way to redeem that. I honestly thought that living with us would be a blessing for him, but I think it's only made it worse. He might have been better off going to a foster home."

"Why? He had a chance to play football and to be in an amazing family—"

"But we're not an amazing family, Noelle. We're a normal family, and right now, we're a broken family." She didn't look at Noelle as she said it, the words soft and rough in her throat. "My boys had a big fight right before Eden's wedding. Casper left and Owen is AWOL and . . . My worst fear is that Owen and Casper end up like my sister and me."

"They won't."

Ingrid shook her head. "They might. If only I knew how to fix it."

Noelle slid her hand over Ingrid's arm. "I don't think you're supposed to."

"I'm the mom. Of course I'm supposed to." She set down the phone. "I always thought I was this amazing mother. I cooked and cleaned and cheered and created a safe haven for the kids. Now . . . now they're gone, and although I knew it was coming, I feel a little . . ."

"Rejected?"

"Betrayed. By life. By God, maybe. I did everything right, I thought. So why don't I have a perfect family?"

"Because our children are destined to leave us from the moment they're born. And the paths they walk are theirs, not ours. We can only give them a place to come home, stop in, find comfort. But we can't walk their journey for them. Eventually they have to stand before God by themselves."

Ingrid saw the grief of Noelle's words in her eyes. Her own daughter had walked that path, was already standing before God. She squeezed Noelle's hand.

"Even Mary had to let her child go," Noelle went on. "You have to wonder, as Mary watched Jesus on the cross, did she look back and ask herself if she had made a mistake? God had told her she would be the mother of the Savior. You can't get more devastated than Mary, watching her Son—the Savior—die."

Ingrid watched Ellie carry more wings to the children's church area.

"But Jesus' path wasn't for Mary to determine. Her greatest ability as a mother was to be His mother. To love Him, nurture Him, care for Him. She embraced her destiny, then let Him go to embrace His. You have to let your children embrace theirs. Including Romeo."

"He's not really my child."

"Not before. And maybe not tomorrow. But right now?" Noelle finished off her tea. "By the way, have you tried asking Darek and Ivy to play Mary and Joseph?"

Darek and Ivy! Had she? She thought she'd mentioned it, but . . .

Ivy picked up on the second ring. "Hey, Mom, what's up?"

The cold snap of the season was happening right here, two days before Christmas, in his own house.

John came downstairs to an empty kitchen—no coffee

brewing, no gingerbread candle flickering to lend ambience to the room. No holiday ribbon twining over the tops of the cupboards, clove-decorated oranges on display on the table, pine boughs on the mantel. No stockings at the hearth, wreath on the door, or eighteen-foot tree towering to the peak in the living room.

The place had all the Christmas cheer of a July afternoon.

His wife had given up.

As John walked over to the coffeepot and searched for a filter, found the cupboards bare, he knew he couldn't let that happen. He might have made a mess of their relationship with Romeo, but . . . Well, he couldn't help but believe he'd made the right choice.

Romeo needed to man up and deal with that.

He found a few old coffee beans in the freezer, ground them, and set up the pot to brew. Then he headed upstairs and pounded on Romeo's door. Opened it when he got no answer.

Romeo slept like a tornado, ripping out his sheets, his quilt wrapped in a stranglehold around him. His bare feet, however, stuck out the bottom. Butterscotch, from beside him on the bed, lifted her head.

"Romeo. Get up."

The kid lifted his head, his hair a messy bramble. "What?"

"You have exactly seven minutes to get dressed and meet me downstairs. And dress warm."

He shut the door, heeded his own words, and was pouring himself a cup of coffee in a travel mug when Romeo appeared, pulling on one of Owen's old sweaters. He gave John a dirty look as he headed to the fridge.

"Shake it off, son, because it's time we added some Christmas cheer to the house."

Romeo frowned at him. But John ignored him. He scooped food into Butter's bowl, then told Romeo, "Find us a saw from the garage. I'll meet you outside."

He didn't look back as he put on his boots, a thick jacket, and a hat and stepped outside.

The snow lifted off in a fine mist as the wind gusted in from the lake. A pristine layer of white left the yard unblemished, and the trees cracked in the wind. Overhead, the clouds hung low, the sky pale.

They just might have a Christmas Eve blizzard, if he knew his Minnesota weather.

Butter trotted out, barking, scooping up snow. Romeo shut the door behind him, wearing Casper's old jacket, boots, and a green knit cap. He trudged to the garage and returned with a saw.

"Why do I need a saw?"

"Because you're going to find us a Christmas tree."

For the first time in three weeks, a spark broke through the sullen pain in Romeo's eyes.

"We have to take a little hike, but it'll be worth it. C'mon."

Butter jumped ahead of them, her legs crashing through the snow. Biting at drifts, barking.

So maybe Ingrid had been right about Butter too. He couldn't imagine the holidays without their family dog.

He followed the shore toward the end of the lake, across the meadow where the burned forest turned lush and full—where Darek had helped lay down a fire line. Here, evergreens flourished, and John had been given carte blanche to harvest his tree from this privately held land.

"Okay, Romeo, find us a tree."

The boy stood surveying the woods. "Really? I can pick any tree?"

"Preferably something we can carry and that isn't taller than the living room ceiling."

Again, the spark in Romeo's eyes, and this time, it

stuck. He began to wander through the forest, shaking snow off trees, inspecting them one by one.

He pointed out a couple and listed their merits as Butter circled around them.

Finally, "I think this one is good." He stood next to an eighteen-foot tree, the lowest branches ten feet around.

"That's a big tree."

"Maybe we just cut it from here." He reached up, indicated the spot. "The bottom branches are rusty anyway. We'll leave the dead parts and just take the top."

"I like it. Saw it down."

"Me?"

"You're carrying the saw." John stepped back, watched Romeo's efforts to hack at the tree. "Can I give you a hint?"

Romeo glanced at him.

"Try cutting it at an angle. Make a wedge. It'll be easier to cut."

Romeo adjusted his saw and the tree came down. It bounced as it landed, the snow puffing off it. John held the tree while Romeo sawed off the lower branches. Then he sawed the trunk again to the right height.

"Okay, grab the back and let's go."

John picked up the front and began to carry. Butter's barks in the distance echoed in the chilly air, and as he walked, surrounded by the rich piney scent of the fallen evergreen, the quiet stirred up memories of hauling home the family tree with his boys.

Four sets of feet all masked by an eighteen-foot tree.

Yeah, he missed that. Or not, because here he was, continuing the tradition with Romeo. He could hear the kid huffing out breath behind him.

"I'll open the patio door, and you feed it in to me," John said.

They wedged the massive tree through the door off the deck. Then Romeo fetched the tree stand and helped John set it up in the great room.

"We'll have to run fishing wire from the tree to the railing to help hold it," John said and sent Romeo back to the garage for wire and a ladder.

Thirty minutes later, they studied their work. "It's a great tree," Romeo said, all hint of pout vanished from his face.

"You picked us a good one," John said.

Romeo gave him a smile, something honest, and it had the ability to ease the terrible knot in John's chest. "Let's get the lights and ornaments."

John went to the basement, dug around, and found the packages of Christmas lights. He handed them out to Romeo, then rooted for the boxes of ornaments.

For years, Ingrid had given each child an ornament for Christmas until they each had a substantial collection. He found Owen's, Casper's, and Amelia's boxes, but no trace of Eden's, Grace's, or Darek's.

He returned upstairs and set the boxes on the counter. Romeo stood on the ladder, stringing lights.

John opened the boxes. It seemed almost sacrilegious to put the ornaments on the tree without the kids.

Romeo climbed off the ladder. "It looks a little . . . bare. Maybe we need more lights."

John stepped back. Outside, shadows pressed against the windows, the gray sky and the northern latitude conspiring to turn the day dark even in midafternoon. Yeah, despite his hopes, the evergreen hadn't exactly made the home magical.

It lacked something. But it was a start, right?

The door opened, and he heard stomping, then the sound of Ingrid dropping her purse. She came into the entryway. Stopped.

And for a moment, so did time as John saw her face change, the years scrolling back to that first Christmas, the one where he'd chopped down their first tree, dragged it home through the woods, draped lights around it at a haphazard angle, hoping to impress his new wife.

She advanced into the room, looking so pretty it could make him ache with the knowledge that she belonged to him. She wore her hair pulled back in a red headband, a white shirt under a red vest, a pair of glittering candy canes dangling from her ears. Corny and sweet in one devastating package. He'd forgotten that about her too.

"Wow," she said.

"You like it?" Romeo asked.

She smiled. "I like it."

For one shiny, bright, perfect moment, everything fit. Like puzzle pieces, finally fixing in place.

Maybe John could resurrect this Christmas season after all.

And then—"Hey, where's Butter?" Romeo looked around as if noticing her absence for the first time.

Ingrid frowned. "Was she outside with you?"

John nodded. "She's probably just chasing squirrels."

Except the wind had begun to howl, his Christmas Eve storm arriving early. Ingrid went to the sliding door, opened it. Whistled. Called.

The wind and snow swirled in at her feet, and still she didn't shut the door.

"I'm sure she's fine," John said, but even he heard the tremor in his voice.

"I'm going out to look for her," Ingrid said.

Which meant that he was too.

Romeo shoved his boots on in silence. John handed him a flashlight and they trudged back out into the cold.

CHAPTER 10

INGRID NEVER THOUGHT she'd say this, but . . . "John, please drive faster."

John gripped the wheel of the Caravan with his gloved hands, ice still caking his pants where he'd plowed through the drifts with her as they searched for Butter. "It's icy, Ingrid. I'm going as fast as I can."

She nodded. Looked out the window at the blades of snow dicing the night. It wasn't his fault.

Not John's fault.

He didn't know that Butter couldn't run outside immediately after eating or that the cold would strain her breathing.

He didn't know or maybe . . . didn't care.

She closed her eyes. Not true. He cared.

Ingrid glanced behind her to where Butter lay, her head on Romeo's lap, her breathing labored. "How is she?"

Romeo had his jaw clenched as if to keep from crying. She didn't blame him. Seeing Butter struggling to make it to the house, her howls echoing in the night, had torn Ingrid asunder. Thankfully, John had picked Butter up in his strong arms and headed straight for the Caravan. Ingrid had dialed the vet from her cell phone as they careened into the night.

"Her stomach keeps getting bigger, and she's whining," Romeo said.

"I thought the doc said this wouldn't happen again if she had surgery," John said darkly. "That's why we spent all that money—"

"It's rare, but yes, it can happen again. We had to be careful . . . feed her a mixture of foods, not let her run immediately after eating, feed her more than once a day." And he would know that if he'd gone with her to pick up Butter after her surgical stay.

No. She wouldn't blame him.

They pulled up to the vet's office. Kate was waiting outside, her jacket on, the light a blur in the wind.

Romeo scooped Butter up and hopped out of the Caravan as John threw it into park. Ingrid followed Romeo inside.

He settled Butter on the stainless steel table. Stroked her fur. "Shh, Butter, it's going to be okay."

"Hello, Romeo," Kate said as she reached for her stethoscope.

Ingrid stopped breathing as Kate listened to Butter's heart. Kate gently probed Butter's stomach just as John came into the room.

"I'd need X-rays, but it seems as though Butter has a gastric torsion again."

"I thought surgery would solve that," John said.

"It almost always does. But perhaps one or two of the surgical tacks failed. She's an old dog, too, and who knows but she didn't heal properly." Kate pressed her fingers against Butter's femoral artery. "We could try to relieve the gases again, but I'm afraid she'd go into cardiac arrest."

"Yes, please. Relieve the pressure."

"Ingrid—"

"John, listen, we have to help her—"

"And then what? More surgery?" He turned to Kate. "She'd have to have surgery again, right?"

"Yes."

Romeo buried his face in Butter's fur.

"But she arrested in surgery last time, and I fear her heart won't take it."

"So we try—"

"Ingrid."

"What? This is our dog, and we love her."

"And she's suffering. Do you want her to continue to suffer?"

"No! Of course not but . . ."

Romeo raised his eyes, so much pain in them that she couldn't breathe. "Please," he said.

She wanted to weep.

John turned to Romeo, putting his hands on the boy's shoulders. "I'm so sorry, Romeo. I know you love her."

Romeo shrugged him away and pushed past him out of the room.

Ingrid walked over to Butter, took her face in her hands, and touched her forehead to the dog's, inhaling the sweet smell of her fur. "Can you give her something to breathe easier?"

"I'll give her a sedative. And some medication for her heart. But it won't stop the inevitable."

Ingrid ran her hands beside Butter's head, rubbed her ears. Butter moaned, and Ingrid saw Kate draw out a needle from her skin. "I'll be right back," Kate said, leaving her intentions unsaid.

Ingrid looked at John. He stood away, hands in his pockets, a grim slash to his mouth.

"I'm not ready," she said.

John stepped toward her, but she held up her hand.

"What? Ingrid, you know it's time."

She closed her eyes, her own breathing labored. When she opened her eyes, a strange, dark churning began in her chest.

"No . . . John, I can't."

He stepped closer, put his hands on her shoulders. "Honey, I know how much you love Butter. But she's just a dog—"

"She's more than a dog. She's family. She's . . . my last child."

She closed her eyes again, turning away from him. "She . . . she's the child I wanted to have but . . . you stole from me."

Silence, and she couldn't believe those words had actually emerged.

Then, "I don't understand."

She hardly did either, but, "John, I . . . If I let Butter go, then it's just you and me. And I have to figure out how to forgive you for that."

His own breathing had deepened, his face wrecked with confusion.

Her voice shook. "Listen. I am so grateful for our six amazing children, and I know a woman in my position shouldn't want more, but the fact is, I wasn't ready to say good-bye to that part of my life. Maybe we would have decided—together—that God was shutting that door. But you just took matters into your own hands."

Her voice dropped. "Yeah, we'd talked about it before I got pregnant, but we'd never decided. Not really. And then you practically ran to the doctor only two weeks after we lost Benjamin. You didn't ask; you simply took charge, and . . . I felt bullied into the decision. I could barely think straight, and then suddenly . . . it was done."

Ingrid wiped her cheek. "If Butter dies, then I have to figure out how . . ." She pressed a hand to her mouth, trying to force out the words. "How to live with you. How to stop being so angry with you. I thought I was over it, but . . . but I'm not. And somehow I have to figure out how to forgive you. How to love you again, anyway."

He didn't move, and for a second, neither did she. Just the rise and fall of their breathing as she stared at him. At the terrible truth she hadn't wanted to believe.

"You stopped trusting God. And I . . . I stopped trusting you."

His mouth tightened. Thankfully, he didn't reach for her. But his eyes glistened, and in a dark, nearly hidden place inside Ingrid, something howled when a tear dropped down his cheek.

"Why didn't you tell me?"

"Why did I have to?" she whispered.

Kate came back into the room, holding a tray with a vial and needle. "I'm so sorry."

Ingrid wiped her cheek fast, hard. "We should get Romeo."

"He's out back with the puppies."

"Leave him," John said. He put his hand on Butter's body, then bent down to meet her eyes. They remained closed. "You were a good dog, Butterscotch." He kissed her between her eyes. Stood. "It's up to Ingrid."

Ingrid looked at Kate and nodded. She clenched her teeth, watching as Kate inserted the needle. "How long will it be?"

"About a minute."

A minute. Ingrid stooped and took Butter's head in her hands, rubbing the soft skin inside her ears. Butter moaned and opened her eyes. Found Ingrid's.

"I love you, Butter," Ingrid whispered, but the words didn't quite make it out.

And then Butter closed her eyes.

Ingrid leaned her head against the dog's belly, listening to her breath until it finally stopped.

"It's too cold outside to bury her," she heard John say, somewhere behind the thundering of her pulse.

"We can take care of her," Kate said quietly.

Ingrid closed her eyes. Bit her lip. Breathed out a long breath.

Then she stood and walked out of the room, leaving Butter on the table behind her.

No doubt Ingrid was right.

John hadn't a prayer of fixing the problems between them. He couldn't exactly go back in time and . . .

Frankly he couldn't get past the idea that he had been right.

For two weeks after the day he'd found his wife in a pool of blood in the bathroom, after he'd rushed her to the ER, after they'd lost Benjamin, after he'd been shaken at his life unraveling before his eyes, he'd watched his wife descend into darkness. So with resolve in his heart, he headed to the doctor.

Because he—they—had six children to raise. Six children who needed their mother. And John couldn't bear the thought of losing her.

If Butter dies, then I have to figure out how . . . to love you again.

He hardly slept, those words seeping into his chest like poison.

At one point, he rolled onto his side, watching the night outline his wife. The desire to rest his hand on her hip, roll her over to himself, try to comfort her, nearly overtook him.

He rose in the darkness of 4 a.m., brewed a cup of coffee, then found Butter's bowl and dog bed and took them out to the garage, hiking back through knee-high drifts.

The blizzard had died with the night, leaving only waves of snow across the deck, the lake a pristine ocean of white.

He hitched the plow to his truck and started in his driveway, clearing a path, then drove into town.

At the station, he climbed into the John Deere, finished his coffee in the thermos, and headed out into Deep Haven, clearing the roads, the snow peeling off his plow in curls of cream, banked in unblemished piles as the sun rose glorious and bronze over the horizon.

If I let Butter go, then it's just you and me. And I have to figure out how to forgive you for that.

Why hadn't she told him?

He parked the plow at the station, then took the truck to the church and cleared the lot. Finally he dug out the manger scene, cleaning it off, and plugged in the heaters.

He drove home with the sun still low, simmering across the icy lake, and thawed out in his living room, staring at their barren tree. He tried to rearrange a few ornaments to hide the empty places, to no avail.

Ingrid trod down the stairs an hour later. She said nothing as she brewed new coffee. Then she cracked eggs and stirred up waffle mix. The smell turned the room familiar, and he walked over to the counter, sat down.

She didn't look at him as she forked out a waffle and handed it to him on a plate.

"Ingrid—"

"I need to get over to the church and set up for the Nativity this afternoon. I have a million things to do—including finding wise men. I can't believe I forgot to cast them." She set the syrup in front of him, then headed upstairs.

He ate in the quiet, missing Butter's nudge on his knee, asking for a bite of waffle.

Ingrid left the house before Romeo rose, and John didn't ask what they might be doing for supper, why the annual wild-rice soup didn't simmer on the stove or why the smell of fresh buns baking didn't fragrance the house.

He was standing, staring out the window, lost in himself, when he heard Romeo rise.

"Um, are these waffles for me?"

Two cold waffles sat on a plate on the counter.

John nodded. "Heat them in the microwave."

He heard the appliance running. Apparently Romeo could take care of himself. Perhaps they all could.

Romeo stirred his waffles through syrup. "Are we going to the live Nativity thing?"

John didn't feel like going anywhere. Still, he nodded.

"Do you think . . . ?" Romeo made a face. For the first time, John noticed his eyes were red, even puffy. "Do you think dogs go to heaven?"

John slid onto a stool. Oh, boy. "I think God loves animals, but the truth is, I don't know the answer to that question. I think we'll have to wait and see." He rested a hand on Romeo's shoulder.

Romeo stared at his waffle, blinking. "Uncle John,

do you think . . . do you think I'll go to heaven when I die?"

Oh. He didn't know why, but the words became a fist in his chest, and he couldn't breathe.

You might consider that you're one of the few father figures he's ever had. Nate's words rattled through him.

"That's a great question, Romeo. And the answer is God loves you, and He wants you to be with Him in heaven. That's the point of Christmas."

Romeo bit his lip. Let out a shuddering breath. Nodded.

John wrapped his arm around the boy's shoulders, his voice thick. "You know, God is just a prayer away. Right there. All you have to do is say you need Him."

Romeo wiped a thumb across his eye.

Oh, God, I'm so sorry I didn't want this kid. This son of Yours. Thank You for giving him to me, for making me realize, again, the gift of being a father.

He, too, wiped his eye, dislodging the moisture there. In fact, it could be that Romeo gave John and Ingrid more than they had given him.

When the phone rang, John got up, found it on the sofa.

"Hey, Dad. . . . Uh, Ivy and I can't do this Nativity

thing today. She's . . . she's not feeling well and . . ." Darek's voice wavered, and John lowered himself onto the sofa.

"What are you talking about?"

"Mom asked Ivy and me to be in the Nativity scene today, but she's throwing up and cramping. . . . I . . . I don't know what to do."

Panic. John heard it in Darek's voice, and it peeled back time to his own moment, standing in the Deep Haven ER, waiting . . . fearing.

Yeah, maybe he hadn't acted out of responsibility but panic when he decided they wouldn't have any more children.

The knowledge turned his voice raw.

"Darek, listen. Don't worry about the live Nativity. I'll take care of it. We're leaving right now to get Tiger. You be ready to take Ivy to the ER."

"Dad . . . do you think she's going to lose the baby?"

"I don't know, Darek. I do know that it's not in your hands. Don't panic. Just pray. That's your job."

That's your job. The words pinged inside him, registered, hung on as he went upstairs to change, hollering at Romeo to do the same.

Darek met him at the apartment door with Tiger, a backpack, and a grim look.

"Hey, Tiger, want to sleep over tonight?" John asked.

"But what about Santa? How will he find me? I don't have a stocking at your house."

"He'll find you, kiddo," John said. He ran in and retrieved Tiger's homemade stocking from the hearth. "We got this," he said as Darek shut the door.

They drove to the church and unloaded Tiger with the other children getting ready to don wings. A wreath hung at the apex of the entrance, and a trail of lights in paper bags surrounded the portico he'd cleaned.

Someone had layered straw on the ground, but the heaters had even thawed a semicircle of snow outside, right down to the grass. A layer of light snow blanketed the top of the stable, but inside, it looked cozy enough to . . . well, host the baby Jesus.

Something even the original Joseph might have approved of.

Inside the church, he found chaos. Edith and her hospitality crew decorated the tables with plates of cookies as a crew of mothers helped their children don angel wings.

Romeo headed over to a gated Sunday school room. Tiger tugged at John's hand. "Grandpa—there's puppies!"

John released him, then followed him to see. Inside the

room, puppies from the shelter frolicked with a handful of children, Kate in the middle, minding the fun.

She met John's eye. "It was Romeo's idea," she said. "He called me about an hour ago and I thought, why not?"

John looked at Romeo. "Really?"

Romeo lifted a shoulder. "Aunt Ingrid was having trouble getting enough animals."

"John, what are you doing here?"

He turned to find Ingrid holding a pair of broken wings and tape.

"Did you find your wise men?"

She frowned, shook her head, then glanced at Tiger. "What's going on? Where are Darek and Ivy?"

John stood there, the words caught in his chest. "Romeo, can you help Tiger with his wings?"

"Sure thing, Uncle John."

"And then come and find me because you're going to be a wise man."

Romeo raised an eyebrow but nodded.

"He's a wise man? Oh . . . okay."

"And . . . honey, we're Mary and Joseph."

"What?"

He grabbed her elbow and brought her into the quiet sanctuary, away from the bustle of the preparations. "I know I should wait to tell you this, and it was going to be a surprise, but . . . Ivy is pregnant and she's a little sick right now, so Darek is bringing her to the hospital."

He didn't let her protest, simply wrapped his arms around her and pulled her to himself. "It'll be okay."

And for a moment, she clung to him. Everything righting itself, her words from last night vanished. For this moment, he could be what she needed.

"Really, you'll be Joseph?" She looked at him, her eyes so beautiful that he felt sick for ever turning her down. He nodded.

"Okay." She pressed her hand to his chest. "The costume is in the nursery, along with your staff and a wool overcoat. I'll go track down the Mary part."

He leaned in to kiss her, but she moved out his arms. Probably not intentionally. He hoped not.

Joseph's attire, along with the wise men's—or man's— hung in the nursery, as Ingrid said. Romeo knocked on the door as John pulled on the tunic.

John handed him his costume, a red flannel jacket with fake rhinestones and a crown. "You know, the most important skill the wise men possessed was their ability to recognize the Savior when they saw him. It's up to you to decide if you're a wise man."

Romeo stared at the robe, back at John, and he couldn't help it—he wrapped an arm around the kid's neck. Just for a second, but long enough.

"I'll be outside, trying not to freeze to death."

The sky had turned dusky with the fall of the afternoon. John found Nate relighting a couple of candles in the bags.

"Wow," Nate said.

"Don't start."

"Hey," Nate said, "I've always thought you'd make a good Joseph."

"Why's that?"

"Because Joseph was a carpenter." He nodded to the stable. "And that fortress could withstand a hurricane."

"Or a blizzard." Ingrid stepped out from the entrance, wearing a blue dress, a white scarf. And mittens.

"Mary might have had mittens," she said.

John smiled at her, and a heat swept through him at the sight of his pretty wife dressed in motherly garb. No one fit the part better.

"We don't have a live baby," Ingrid said, producing a doll in a blanket. She tromped over to the Nativity, putting the baby bundle in the manger. "By the way, I called Darek. They're in the ER, but they think maybe it's just the flu. They're doing an ultrasound."

John stepped up behind her. Put his hand on her shoulder.

Don't panic. Just pray. His own words reverberated through him. If only he'd had such a voice sixteen years ago.

He took his position behind Mary as she sat by the manger.

The heat blasted out, the coils red-hot behind him. He hadn't realized what a tight fit it would be, but the enclave was warm. Not exactly cozy, but bearable.

The church choir stood under the entrance and began to hum. Cars pulled up, and a meager handful of community members stopped to take pictures or stand and watch, singing with the choir.

John shivered despite the heater and backed up just a little. Maybe they could go in for cookies early if no one else showed up.

The angels filtered out and stood on the hay around the manger while parents snapped pictures. Tiger waved to him, and John winked.

In his brain flashed a memory of Casper and Owen as angels. To his memory, they'd gotten in a wrestling match and come home wet and frozen.

Then the shepherds appeared—a handful of grade

school boys dressed in bathrobes. Finally the wise man. Romeo approached carrying a gold box.

"I can't believe I forgot the wise men," Ingrid said under her breath. "Thanks."

Pastor Dan stood on a hay bale and welcomed everyone.

"The first Christmas wasn't even this well attended," he said. "But the participants were handpicked by God. The shepherds, who were asked simply to believe and to go and worship. The wise men, who recognized the star of Bethlehem before Jesus' arrival and set off on a journey to find Him. Their searching was rewarded with joy. The angels, the trumpeters of glory born on earth. Joseph, the Savior's earthly father, his only job requirement that of listening and obeying God. Being trustworthy. And finally Mary, who trusted God and allowed herself to be used by the Almighty for the good of us all. We invite you tonight to the manger and ask, who are you? Is God asking you to believe? Is He rewarding your search tonight with Himself? Are you here with a heart of joy? Or perhaps you need to listen, to trust and obey. Maybe, however, you're Mary, and God is simply asking you to be willing to say yes to whatever He asks."

He stepped down, and the choir sang a verse of "Silent Night."

John stood there, warm in the enclave.

Perhaps you need to listen, to trust and obey. He found Romeo's eyes on him and remembered his question. Why did God pick Joseph? A simple man who worked with his hands, with the one skill God wanted for raising His Son. The ability to listen.

Not provide. Not protect. Not even lead, but listen, trust, and obey.

Like when God appeared to Joseph in a dream and told him to keep his engagement to Mary. And later, when God told him to move to Egypt in the night to protect Jesus. After that, the dream to return home so Jesus could grow to be the Nazarene, a fulfillment of prophecy.

Listen. Trust. Obey.

You stopped trusting God. And I . . . I stopped trusting you.

Oh. He swallowed hard against a gasp. He *had* stopped trusting God—he'd simply decided that he should be in control, rather than God. He'd held his children in his arms and thought, *I must provide.* But what if God handed him his family and said, *Trust Me; listen and obey*?

He pressed his hand on Ingrid's shoulder. She glanced at him.

He met her eyes, held them, struck by how young and beautiful and immensely blue they still were.

"I'm sorry," he said quietly. His throat tightened. "I'm so sorry."

She blinked and bit her lip. Then her eyes widened and she jumped up. "John! You're on fire!"

CHAPTER 11

AT LEAST NO ONE had to stand out in the cold for an hour.

John's robe had caught fire against the hot coils of the heaters, and as he shrugged it off, flames bit at the edges of the straw. He'd practically picked up Ingrid in his arms and tossed her into the snow. By the time Pastor Dan found the shovel, John and Nathan and a handful of other men had been scooping snow with their bare hands, throwing it onto the flames of the engulfed manger.

The fire streaked into the sky, searing the night and calling out the neighbors. Someone alerted the police and then the volunteer fire department and even the rescue squad, which came in handy when the Bethlehem star affixed above the manger exploded in a shower of glass and sparks.

Parents scattered with their children back into the church, where the EMTs checked for injuries.

Then the newspaper staff showed up with photographers.

Someone must have alerted the Lutheran church prayer chain because the pastor and his wife—not to mention a handful of carolers—arrived, probably straight from the senior center, where they'd been hosting a Christmas Eve service.

A significant portion of the Congregational Church, having been let out of their own Christmas Eve service, showed up to offer moral support. They brought cookies.

In the midst of it all, somehow the puppies escaped, and as more onlookers arrived, a few scampered out into the snowy night. Which brought out the search parties to track them down; then, of course, a few traumatized children who envisioned frozen puppies lost in the snow had to be comforted.

Snow and boots and coats lined the foyer. Ingrid found Tiger and simply fed him cookies, watching the chaos.

No, watching John.

Watching his hands turn red with cold as he tried to keep their church from catching fire. Watching as he donned a turnout coat and boots and joined the crew to douse the flames, stomping out any remaining ash, raking his beautiful manger scene to glowing embers.

Watching as he searched through the snow for lost puppies, warming them in his big hands with towels they'd found in the church kitchen.

She watched as he bore the brunt of more than a few jokes from the cookie-hungry fire personnel. He managed to laugh, his voice loud and low, just a hint of chagrin on his face.

Humble. Patient. Protecting.

He retrieved Tiger, helped him take off his wings, and replaced them with the turnout coat and hat.

Ingrid caught a puppy and hunkered down with it, and that's when John found her. He crouched beside her and handed her a gingerbread man.

"I have to say, honey, your live Nativity just might be the best attended one ever," he said, his face solemn, his blue eyes twinkling.

How she wanted to laugh. Could feel it bubbling up, right under the surface. Oh, John. He could be magnetic and breathtaking and infuriatingly darling and . . . Tears burned her eyes.

Maybe, however, you're Mary, and God is simply asking you to be willing to say yes to whatever He asks.

She'd been asked to love this man. To trust him. Even when he failed her.

She looked away, wiped a finger under her eyes.

John swallowed, the twinkle in his eyes dying. "Let's go home."

"Yes," she said quietly and let John help her off the floor. She returned the puppy, found Tiger and Romeo, and headed out the door.

She managed to pull together some soup and a plate of leftover cookies from church. Then she tucked Tiger onto her lap and read him the Christmas story.

Admittedly, without Butter curled at her feet, she struggled to summon the joy she knew she should feel at the holiday. And Tiger's tears when they told him that Butter had "gone to heaven" only turned the evening somber.

Thankfully, the phone call from Darek updating them on Ivy's condition lightened her grief, but worry settled in again when Darek said they wanted Ivy to stay the night for observation, just to make sure the baby was out of danger.

It all brought back the memory of Benjamin. The joy at being pregnant, the fear when he stopped moving inside her. The moment when she felt her body release him, the blood on the floor, and the hazy hours that followed.

Long after they tucked Tiger in bed, she sat in the family room, rocking, wishing for Butter's fur to run her fingers through.

John and Romeo found a puzzle, something simple they could finish in a night.

After a while, Romeo went to bed. John sat in silence, watching the fire flicker, until finally he left her also.

Maybe, however, you're Mary, and God is simply asking you to be willing to say yes to whatever He asks.

She pulled her legs onto the chair, stared at the tree, lights glistening from the bulbs. Patches of naked green tree remained, but John had waged a worthy battle to cover its bareness with ornaments.

In fact, she couldn't deny the evidence of John's attempt to resurrect Christmas for her, from the trip to Europe to the half-decorated tree, from the Nativity scene to his words today just before the chaos erupted.

I'm sorry.

Oh, how those words had the power to burrow into the wall around her heart, open up fissures and cracks.

I'm so sorry.

She didn't want to hear it. To see his love in a thousand small ways. Because then she'd have to loose her hold on the ember of bitterness, let God heal her heart.

Worse, she'd have to reckon with the truth that she might be just as responsible for the rift in their marriage.

If you love someone, you don't act like they annoy you. You like them, and you try to make them think they're the most important person in the world to you.

Romeo's words had tucked inside, just under her skin, and seeing John in action only uncovered the ugliness. Somehow, over the past few months, she'd stopped loving John. Even liking him. She'd been going through the motions, pretending, masking her wounds.

And when he didn't notice them anyway, they only grew deeper.

But deeper than her pain lingered the truth. She did love John. Loved him so much that sometimes she could weep with the depth of it. And if she were honest . . .

Of course she trusted him. Every day of her life. She simply didn't want to forgive him. She'd preferred to hold on to the anger, the resentment, rather than face the grief of her loss.

But forgiveness just might fix this.

She drew in a long breath, got up, and headed upstairs.

He wasn't asleep as she had supposed. Instead, he stood at the window, still dressed, staring out at the lake.

"I always thought my job was to protect you. To provide

for you. I had no idea doing that would also destroy what we had." He didn't look at her. "I wish I could, but I can't fix this, Ingrid."

She sank down on the bed. "I should have told you how I felt."

To her surprise, he shook his head. Then he turned. A dim light from the bedside table scattered the darkness, and she easily traced his beautiful blue eyes, the look of sadness in them. "And I should have listened to you."

Oh. She didn't know why his admission turned her throat thick and scratchy, but she blinked back the burn in her eyes, fighting the urge to flee.

He came and knelt in front of her, taking her face in his wide, strong hands. "I can't fix it, but I believe God can. I know He can help me be a husband who listens. And I pledge to do that—to listen. To you, to God. To obey and trust God."

A tear dripped down her chin, over his thumb. "I'm sorry I blamed you—"

"But I am to blame. I did this."

She hung her hands on his wrists. "I know. And when you did, I should have forgiven you. Trusted that God could heal me. But . . . I don't know that I wanted to be healed. Or that I should be—should I ever really heal from the loss of our child?"

John found her eyes. "I think healing is different from forgetting. I admit I've been guilty of that too. I'm sorry I tried to fix everything with a dog. Not an inspired move—I get that. But I gave you Butter because I didn't know what else to do. And I got a vasectomy because I was scared. I feared losing you, losing another baby. I was overwhelmed with my life and . . . yeah, I thought it was all up to me to fix it. To take care of us. So I tried to put it behind us when I should have tried to help you heal. I should have leaned into God for courage, instead of reacting in fear."

She closed her eyes, tipping her head forward to touch his. The sense of his presence—strong, warm—flooded through her, shook her.

How she'd missed him.

"You're an amazing mother, Ingrid. Our children are going to be just fine. We need to let them sort this out. And . . ." He backed up, met her eyes again. "Romeo is going to be fine."

"You think so?"

"I know it."

She touched his face, ran her fingers along the stubble. "Perhaps it's a good thing we have such a quiet house this season."

Then she leaned in and kissed him. Softly at first and then with a depth, a passion that came from knowing this man, believing in him. Seeing all the ways he loved her without speaking.

John pulled back, moisture in his eyes. So blue . . . She could remember the first day they landed on her, turned her mouth to dust, and curled desire inside her.

"I love you so much. And I want the next thirty years to be even better than the last."

Ingrid ran her thumbs over his cheekbones. "I believe they will be."

She kissed him again, and this time he didn't pull away, didn't hesitate to hook his arm around her waist, pull her with him onto their bed. She sank into his amazing arms—strong, protective, safe—and found in his embrace the woman she'd been once upon a time. Young. Eager.

Humbled by her destiny and willing to say yes to whatever God—and John—asked.

Christmas arrived with the smells of brewing cider on the stove and homemade cinnamon rolls, the sound of Tiger's laughter.

John slipped on a bathrobe, his slippers, and headed downstairs.

Tiger sat on the floor, surrounded by the decadence of his stocking—Matchbox cars, markers, a LEGO kit, a giant chocolate Santa. He got up and ran to John. "Merry Christmas, Grandpa!"

John swung him in the air, gave him a kiss. "Merry Christmas, Tiger."

He put down Tiger, who turned to Ingrid. "Now can we open presents?"

Ingrid closed the oven after basting the turkey. "Wait until your mommy and daddy get here."

John walked over to her, slipped his arm around her waist, pulled her back against himself, and kissed her neck. "When do I get to open my present?"

She whacked him with a pot holder. "John Christiansen, you got your present." But she turned in his arms, lifting hers to wrap around his neck, and gave him a kiss that promised perhaps he had more waiting for him.

Much more.

"That's gross."

John released his wife to see Tiger staring at them. The boy covered his face with his hands, giggling.

"Have you talked to Darek or Ivy yet today?" John asked.

Ingrid disentangled herself and walked over to the coffeepot. Took down a cup. "Ivy is fine and so is the baby." She poured coffee into the cup and handed it to John. "She was just dehydrated."

"I'm so glad."

"They're waiting for the doctor to discharge her; then they'll be over." She looked at Tiger. "Another grandchild. That feels so . . ."

"Wonderful." John couldn't help it. After the dry spell, the wounds between them, he simply wanted to savor the feeling of having his wife surrender freely in his arms. He reached for her, cupped her cheek, and she smiled into his eyes.

"I think you need to wake up Romeo," she said.

Romeo. He kissed her, then headed upstairs.

The door was closed, but he heard whining, faint and high, as he knocked.

"Just a second—"

John opened the door without waiting. Romeo stood in the middle of the room in a T-shirt and pajama pants, holding a squirming puppy in a blanket.

Oh no. John closed the door behind him. Raised an eyebrow.

"I'm sorry, Uncle John." The puppy shifted in his arms, and the blanket dropped away, showing a wriggling mass of brown-and-white fur and oversize, floppy ears, giant paws. Romeo nearly dropped him, then pulled him to his chest. "He was the runt, and he was so cold, I tucked him in my jacket and sort of . . ."

"Brought him home."

Romeo lifted a shoulder.

The swift, sharp memory of Owen holding a fidgeting Butterscotch could nearly take John's breath away. He walked over to the dog and settled his hand on its head. The animal had blue eyes that searched John's. Oh, boy.

"He won't be any trouble; I promise. And . . . he's a good dog; I know it. I think he just needs someone to care about him and make sure he doesn't get forgotten and hurt and . . . Maybe I could just keep him over Christmas?"

John looked at Romeo, a near man at seventeen. Wide shoulders, sparse blond whiskers layering his chin, his hair too long, and compassion in his eyes. The makings of a hero.

"I think you should keep him longer than that," John said quietly. "I think you need to give him a home."

"Really?"

"Absolutely. We'll go over later and officially adopt him from the shelter. Merry Christmas, Romeo."

Romeo smiled then, the fear breaking free, his eyes clear, bright. "Merry Christmas, Uncle John."

Indeed. John somehow found his voice. "I think there's breakfast waiting for you. And I'll bet this little guy is hungry."

The puppy tucked himself against Romeo's shoulder, licking his face. John followed him out of the room and down the stairs.

Ingrid looked up at them. Her mouth opened. "Is that a—?"

"A puppy!" Tiger squealed and jumped up from the floor.

"Seriously, John?" she said, but she grinned as Romeo bent down to hand Tiger the puppy.

"Careful now," Romeo said. "He's scared, but he just needs a little TLC." Tiger giggled as the puppy bathed his chin.

"I think Santa left you something," Ingrid said to Romeo, gesturing toward the hearth.

A thick stocking with Romeo's name stitched on the cuff hung from one of the pegs.

He walked over to it. Touched his name, then unhooked the stocking. Brought it to the sofa, where he pulled out a pair of socks. Gloves. Then a hat. And his own chocolate Santa.

He looked up at Ingrid, at John. "I . . ."

"Everybody needs a stocking with their name on it," Ingrid said softly.

Romeo grinned, then reached for his new gloves, trying them on. Tiger ran over with his LEGO kit, the puppy biting at his feet. "Wanna help me build my new LEGO? It's an airplane with propellers!"

"Sure," Romeo said and slid to the floor while Tiger dumped out the pieces. Romeo gathered the pup into his lap.

Ingrid watched them a moment, and John had no doubt that a reel from the past played through her mind. Probably Darek helping Owen, or maybe even Eden and Grace dressing their new Barbie dolls.

Or maybe a vision of the grandchildren they'd have, filling the house with chaos and laughter and joy.

He slipped his arm around her and pulled her close. "We'll call the kids later. But I have an idea. After dinner, would you be open to a small trip on Christmas Day?"

They pulled up to the block-long, three-story brick building, parking in the lot across the street. Snow banked the lot, freshly plowed, and light pooled over a few cars, some covered by a thick layer of snow and ice.

Ingrid took the tinfoil-wrapped container of turkey, stuffing, mashed potatoes, and gravy from the back of the Caravan. Romeo carried a plate of cookies, and John grabbed the wrapped present, something small Ingrid had kept for this kind of moment.

They walked up to the back door, and the security guard buzzed them in, a middle-aged man with kindness on his face. "Upstairs to the left is the foyer. They'll buzz you in."

The place had all the charm of a European boarding school, with the musty cement walls, the scent of institution in the polished marble floors, the stoic furniture. Ingrid perched on the end of a straight chair as the receptionist took their names, then placed a call.

In a moment, she appeared, dressed in jeans and a Hard Rock Cafe T-shirt, her hair long and braided down the back. Thinner than Ingrid remembered, she wore her trials on her face even as it broke into a smile at the sight of her son.

"Romeo!" Kari opened her arms, and he enveloped her in his embrace, standing a whole head taller. As she closed her eyes and clung to him, Ingrid slipped her hand into John's.

He'd listened. Without her even asking, he knew.

Kari released Romeo and turned to Ingrid.

Silence passed between them. Then, "Hey, Sis," Ingrid said.

Kari brushed a tear from her cheek. "You didn't have to come all the way down here for Christmas—"

"Yes, we did," John said quietly. "You're family, and we didn't like the idea of you spending it alone."

She gave a half smile, shrugged, and Ingrid recognized the gesture.

"We brought turkey and stuffing. Mom's recipe." She reached out and pulled Kari into a hug.

Her sister resisted a moment, then sank into the embrace. "Thank you," she whispered.

"It was John's idea," Ingrid whispered back.

Kari pulled away, looked at John. "I'm so grateful for all you've done. I know it's been a lot of trouble, but I—"

"No trouble at all, Kari."

She wiped her cheek. "The doctors say I could probably be out by the end of January. Can you keep him until then?"

John glanced at Romeo. "He'll always have a home with us."

Ingrid took John's hand again as the receptionist buzzed them into the facility. Romeo walked with his arm around his mom's shoulder, his voice lifting as he told her about football and the live Nativity, his Christmas stocking, Butter, and his new puppy, Bud.

She gave John's hand a squeeze. "And what exactly are we going to do with Romeo and Bud when we visit Amelia in Prague?"

"Don't toy with me, woman."

"Oh, John," she said, turning to him, pulling him into her embrace, laughing. "I'm just getting started."

Dear family and friends,

A warm Christmas greeting from snowy northern Minnesota!

As many of you know, our property was devastated a year ago in a forest fire. We watched as the flames took our cabins, our history, our livelihood.

I had no idea it might be the beginning of a string of farewells.

John and I found ourselves—expectedly, of course—with an empty nest this year. And while I'd prepared for it, the swiftness with which it swept into my life, like the turning of the seasons from autumn to the stiff winds of winter, took my breath away.

We bid Amelia good-bye at the airport in Minneapolis, bound for a year of education in Prague, and I returned to the emptiness and winter in my heart.

Not that I didn't have joy. With Darek and

Ivy's wedding Memorial Day weekend, and Eden's celebration of marriage to Jace Jacobsen (the former captain of the St. Paul Blue Ox who is now on their coaching staff), I delighted in welcoming two new children to the family. We're thrilled that Grace, our family chef, has also found her true love, as she is engaged to Maxwell Sharpe. (You know him as a wing for the Blue Ox.)

However, we also said good-bye to Casper as he headed to Roatán, Honduras, to seek treasure in an archaeological dig, and to Owen, who is finding new footing.

And then we lost our beloved Butterscotch. It felt like too many good-byes.

But that's the magic of a good-bye—it makes way for something new. An unexpected hello.

We love living in the north because the seasons are ever changing. But there also remains a constant. It's a miracle how, when an evergreen burns, the pinecones burst open, dropping seeds into the fertile soil of the charred land. Saplings now edge our property, sprouts of green against the white landscape.

In the wake of good-byes, life endures. Even flourishes.

New life came first in the form of our nephew Romeo, who stayed with us this fall and during the Christmas season. And then in the news that John and I will be welcoming another grandbaby—Darek and Ivy are expecting in the spring.

But more than that, all this sudden room in our lives allowed John and me to take a full breath. To find ourselves in the midst of the winter landscape surrounded by beautiful, tender evergreens, look at each other, and say, "Hello. You're still here?"

Indeed, we are. Flourishing in the fertile soil of our years together.

We're headed to Europe this Valentine's Day to renew our vows, leaving the newly reopened resort in our eldest son's capable hands. And then back to the resort for a new season.

Come and visit us! We're waiting with a warm hello.

> *With love from Evergreen Resort,*
> *Ingrid and John Christiansen*

ABOUT THE AUTHOR

Susan May Warren is the bestselling, Christy and RITA Award–winning author of more than forty novels whose compelling plots and unforgettable characters have won acclaim with readers and reviewers alike. She served with her husband and four children as a missionary in Russia for eight years before she and her family returned home to the States. She now writes full-time as her husband runs a resort on Lake Superior in northern Minnesota, where many of her books are set.

Susan holds a BA in mass communications from the University of Minnesota. Several of her critically acclaimed novels have been ECPA and CBA bestsellers, were chosen as Top Picks by *Romantic Times*, and have won the RWA's Inspirational Reader's Choice contest and the American Christian Fiction Writers' prestigious Carol Award. Her novel *You Don't Know Me* won the 2013 Christy Award, and six of her other books have also been finalists. In addition to her writing, Susan loves to teach and speak at women's events about God's amazing grace in our lives.

For exciting updates on her new releases, information about her previous books, and more, visit her website at ww.susanmaywarren.com.

DISCUSSION QUESTIONS

1. At the beginning of *Evergreen*, John is working on a plan to surprise Ingrid with a trip to Europe. What did you think of his idea . . . and Ingrid's reaction to his proposal? Have you ever planned a big surprise for someone you love—or been on the receiving end of one? How did it turn out?

2. John and Ingrid have very different feelings about the approaching empty nest season in their lives. While John is excited about new opportunities, Ingrid struggles to let go of her children and wrestles with doubts about how her family has turned out. How have you approached new phases in your own life? With excitement? Anticipation? Regret? Fear?

3. When the Christiansens' dog, Butterscotch, gets sick, John and Ingrid initially disagree over whether to spend their savings on her surgery. Whose perspective did you agree with? Why?

4. Romeo has grown up believing the Nativity story is a fairy tale. To help him understand the real-life story, John encourages Romeo to imagine himself in Joseph's position, dealing with the news of Mary's pregnancy. Have you ever pictured the Christmas story through the eyes of the participants? Whom do you most relate to? How does John himself end up connecting to Joseph's role?

5. Although John and Ingrid have what most would consider a happy marriage, their past together contains some deep wounds. Ingrid is surprised to find her anger at John resurfacing when she thought she'd gotten over it years ago. Is there a difference between moving on from something in the past and truly resolving it? How does Ingrid ultimately put the past to rest?

6. John offers to sign Romeo's emancipation papers, allowing him to enter the military, but is surprised by Romeo's less-than-enthusiastic reaction. Why does Romeo respond the way he did?

7. Both Butterscotch and Romeo fill a place in Ingrid's heart left empty by the loss of her last child. Was this a healthy way to deal with her grief? Has there been

a time when you tried to replace a loss in a similar way—or had someone try to replace it for you, as John did in giving Butter to Ingrid?

8. Facing a Christmas without most of her family around, Ingrid is reluctant to celebrate or even to decorate her house. Can you think of a celebration that didn't live up to what you hoped, or of a tradition—like the live Nativity—that seemed to be dying out over time? What traditions have you let go of as life changed? Which have you held on to? Why?

9. John has always believed that protecting Ingrid is part of his job—in everything from making decisions about having more children to keeping her from getting her heart broken when Romeo leaves. But Ingrid tells him, "We can't live our lives trying to protect ourselves from getting hurt. And you can't live your life trying to protect me." When have you struggled with a desire to protect someone you love or to protect yourself from getting hurt?

10. As he walks through the Christmas story with those gathered for the live Nativity, Pastor Dan suggests, "Maybe . . . you're Mary, and God is simply asking

you to be willing to say yes to whatever He asks." How does this hit home for Ingrid? What would it mean for you to say yes to whatever God asked?

MORE GREAT FICTION
· FROM ·
SUSAN MAY WARREN

THE **DEEP HAVEN**
NOVELS
Happily Ever After
Tying the Knot
The Perfect Match
My Foolish Heart
The Shadow of Your Smile
You Don't Know Me
Hook, Line & Sinker: A Deep Haven novella

TEAM HOPE
SERIES
Flee the Night
Escape to Morning
Expect the Sunrise
Waiting for Dawn: A Team Hope novella

THE **PJ SUGAR**
SERIES
Nothing but Trouble
Double Trouble
Licensed for Trouble

THE **NOBLE LEGACY**
SERIES
Reclaiming Nick
Taming Rafe
Finding Stefanie

STAND-ALONE TITLES
The Great Christmas Bowl

www.susanmaywarren.com

CP0790